THAT'S HOW IT WORKS

THAT'S HOW IT WORKS

THIRTY YEARS OF FICTION FROM HUB CITY PRESS

HUB CITY PRESS
SPARTANBURG, SC

Design Lead: Meg Reid
Hub City Editor: Katherine Webb-Hehn
Cover Art: Becca Barnet
Copy Editor: Tessa Carvalho
Managing Editor: Kate McMullen
Marketing Assistant: Julie Jarema
Proofreaders: Madeline Fiema, Tharyn Stribling

Library of Congress Cataloging-in-Publication Data

Names: Webb-Hehn, Katherine editor | Reid, Meg writer of introduction
Title: That's how it works : 30 years of fiction from Hub City Press /
editor, Katherine Webb-Hehn; introduction by Meg Reid.
Description: Spartanburg, South Carolina : Hub City Press, 2025.
Identifiers:
LCCN 2025019128
ISBN 9798885740647 paperback
Subjects:
LCSH: Short stories, American—21st century
LCGFT: Short stories
Classification:
LCC PS648.S5 T47 2025
DDC 813/.010806—dc23/eng/20250508
LC record available at https://lccn.loc.gov/2025019128

First edition | Printed in the USA

HUB CITY PRESS
153 North Spring Street
Spartanburg, SC 29306
864.577.9349 | www.hubcity.org

Table of contents

Introduction
Meg Reid

In 1995, three Spartanburg writers set out to make their city a center for the literary arts. Betsy Teter, John Lane, and Gary Henderson sat in a coffee shop in downtown Spartanburg, a small city in South Carolina that, like so many other towns in the South and nationwide, had lost its textile industry because of automation and international competition. The view out the window of that shop was a crumbling, half-demolished, weedy, and forgotten place. The mass layoffs and mill closures hit the Upstate at a level previously unseen. The mood in town was grim. Job prospects weren't stellar and the general loss of income, purpose, and community had rattled the small town. These three writers asked: What, if anything, was the job of an artist or writer at this moment?

The loss of industry was more than just the 25,000 jobs—it was, as historian Cal Preston Bedenbaugh argues, like a "death in the family," a de-humanizing moment for an area whose identity and community structure were built around being the textile manufacturing capital of the world. Abandoned mills, their smokestacks rising like empty flagpoles, dotted the landscape. Downtowns slowly drained of people and businesses. Betsy wrote the following for *Orion* Magazine in 1998:

> Three writers sat in the window of a nearby coffee shop in May of 1995 and drew a plan on a napkin to enlist other local authors to write about the experience of living in Spartanburg. We didn't know each other well back then, but we shared a belief that our community, like many others, was losing its sense of place, that it was in danger of being buried under a gaudy mix of strip shopping centers, chain stores, industrial parks, and asphalt. We saw our traditional landscape vanishing, not only the old buildings, but the farms and forests and peach orchards, too. Disappearing along with them was a sense of communality and shared destiny.

The founders of the Hub City Writers Project set a lofty goal: to capture Spartanburg's stories in this moment, both to counter the silencing effect of the losses and preserve its history for future generations. They intentionally looked to the past for inspiration. They chose the name "Hub City" as a nod to Spartanburg's history as a vital railroad hub during the South's industrial heyday, while "Writers Project" referenced the Federal Writers' Project of the 1930s, when the U.S. government recognized the value of arts, culture, and literary recordkeeping in times of strife and put writers to work in their communities. They sought to redefine what it means to inhabit, or as they put it, "re-inhabit" the city where they lived.

The first book Hub City Press published, *Hub City Anthology*, was a place-based collection of personal essays and art about the experience of living in Spartanburg. Filled with seemingly mundane stories, it charmingly defined the town as, "Sad, proud, and bit eccentric." This book launched not just the Press, but a deeply egalitarian ethos that would sustain us for the next three decades. It's always been essential to our mission that our authors are librarians, teachers, homemakers, urban planners, journalists, programmers, activists, and organizers. Our success is proof that there's no one correct way to make a literary culture; a thriving literary culture doesn't require arts benefactors or corporate underwriting or even an immense population center. Every place has a story to tell. Every place is full of storytellers.

And we've grown—not just in reach, but in impact. Today, Hub City Press publishes eight to ten titles annually, with a staff of eleven housed in a renovated historic Masonic Temple on Spartanburg's town square and an editorial office just down the street. From that little anthology came a slew of other books about Spartanburg, the Upstate, and South Carolina, until 2010, when the Press solidified its mission, expanded its footprint and set about to publish only Southern writers. That would include writers with stories in this anthology like Carter Sickels and Ron Rash, George Singleton and Ashleigh Bryant Phillips, as well as poets like Ashley M. Jones, Drew Lanham, and Marlanda Dekine. We remain the only independent press dedicated exclusively to Southern writers and have evolved into the most active and ambitious independent literary publisher in the nation, releasing books by authors from Kentucky to Florida to Texas. Our hallmark is a book that reinterprets, reimagines, or interrogates the modern or historical South.

We've built a nonprofit model that places equal value on an acclaimed publishing program and local community programming. Over the years, we've offered a national fellowship program, a summer writers conference, publishing internships, and youth writing camps. We've donated more than 100,000 books to our local community.

Over the past thirty years, Hub City Press has grown into a cultural engine of the South, leaving a lasting mark on contemporary Southern literature and launching an entirely new generation of writers. Carter Sickels's *The Prettiest Star*—a devastating story of a man returning to his hometown after an AIDS diagnosis—is now a touchstone of queer Appalachian literature. Ashleigh Bryant Phillips's *Sleepovers* draws comparisons to Breece D'J Pancake and Carson McCullers, offering stories that eschew tired rural tropes in favor of clarity, tenderness, and stunning emotional precision. Readers and critics alike celebrate Halle Hill's debut collection, *Good Women*, for its immediacy, humor, and deep generosity of spirit. While we have always prioritized launching debut voices, we've found equal inspiration in reintroducing more established ones—writers like Ron Rash, George Singleton, and Minrose Gwin, whose work continues to shape the Southern literary landscape in vital ways.

It was in this tradition, of honoring the many places, the many people, the many stories of the South, that we decided to publish *That's How It Works: Thirty Years of Fiction from Hub City Press.*

The writers in this collection of short stories share many obsessions. The Southern summer pulses just beneath the surface of these stories—AC units laboring against the heat, sodas sweating through Styrofoam cups, endless car rides, pools as zones of negotiation, and the quiet aches of growing up and growing older. Again and again, these narratives return to themes of grief, memory, and longing—each shaped by the distinct rhythms and contradictions of their place.

In Halle Hill's "Hungry," a teenage girl navigates her father's terminal illness by channeling her grief into calorie counting and the rigid rules of Weight Watchers. In Ron Rash's "French I," a middle school mishap with an Erector Set shadows a man into adulthood. Emily Pease's "Church Retreat, 1975" follows two teenage girls and a drunken veteran praying that nothing goes wrong in a rundown motel room. And in Thomas Pierce's "The Immortal Milkshake," an artificially intelligent chimpanzee debates eternal life with a scientist in the research lab where they're both confined. Characters have meaningful moments at an Elvis festival outside Detroit, the Jaws ride at Universal Studios, and a Houston City Council meeting in a hurricane-wrecked near-future. The stories are tender, sometimes strange, and always precise. Similarly, our cover artist, Becca Barnet, a Spartanburg artist now running the much-lauded Charleston design studio, Sisal Creative, imbues so much deep feeling of both character and setting into those three little lawn chairs. With simple lines, she grounds us in the familiar yet universal environment of the backyard, the front porch, and other places where we meet our community.

We've long argued that our mission isn't to publish work that speaks only to our own region but to instead find stories rooted in place that have resonances far beyond it. The best literature doesn't limit itself to geography; the best literature uses setting as a lens through which to explore universal questions and illuminate deeply human experiences. Maybe the universal condition is that we're all a bit sad, fiercely proud, and a little bit eccentric.

In 2013, five years before I became Publisher, I stepped into the Hub City Bookshop for the first time and was immediately swept up in the whirlwind that was Betsy Teter, then the Press's only employee. Though Spartanburg's downtown was still mostly empty, change was in the air. The city was raffling off empty storefronts and artists were doing pop-up exhibits in vacant lots. A steady stream of international companies moved into the county, transforming it once again into a hub for more modern manufacturing. There was a shared feeling that this scrappiness was our best asset, not an impediment. Betsy had just run a successful capital campaign to renovate the beautiful and historic Masonic Temple on Main Street. Thanks to the individual donations of hundreds of

Spartanburg residents, she transformed dingy law offices into a light-filled independent bookshop and community space.

She told *Publishers Weekly* at the time, "Everybody else in the world was getting out of the bookstore business, so we said, hey, let's get in!" Fifteen years later, Hub City Bookshop is now one of the nation's most established full-service bookshops operated by a literary nonprofit and one of the longest-running businesses in our end of downtown Spartanburg. By the time I arrived, she was shifting her gaze back to the Press—and I did my best to keep up.

I grew up far from any major publishing scene, first in Canada and then in rural Maine. But my small Maine town had an esteemed poetry press in Alice James Books, so I knew early on that transformative publishing could come from anywhere. A belief that literature doesn't have to come from our coasts or biggest cities has guided me ever since. It's why I believe so deeply in the power of decentralization, in building book culture from the ground up, and in staffing our organizations with people whose voices and lived experiences shape the work in meaningful ways.

It's why this anthology includes not only voices from our publishing catalog, but also work by writers like James Yeh, Desiree Evans, and Kelsey Ronan, who came through Hub City residency programs—fifteen years of welcoming authors to Spartanburg to live, write, and work in this community. Perhaps most meaningfully, it features work by our staff, all accomplished writers in their own right. Kate McMullen, who joined us in 2017, has shaped our fiction list with boldness and imagination. She and Christine McSwain contribute stories to this collection, while Julie Jarema offers a comic that hilariously weighs in on how we manage to do so much with such a small team. The anthology's editor, Katherine Webb-Hehn—who came on board in 2020—works closely with our writers, honing their books with unmatched care and commitment in thoughtful collaborations that often span months. It's a reminder that the Hub City Writers Project has always been exactly that: an ongoing and evolving collective project.

I'm writing this at the end of a long, hot summer—one in which books and independent publishing feel more imperiled than ever. Division in our country has eroded communication and fueled a rise in misinformation. We're not listening to each other, and we're not learning from each other. From book challenges and bans to grant terminations and funding threats, it seems each day brings a new obstacle to artmaking and literature.

In this critical moment, independent publishers are more vital than ever because we have an opportunity to work outside of this division. To publish work that explains our current moment but also challenges us to look beyond it. To prioritize care and cultivation over speed and volume, and to advocate for our staff, while introducing new people to this wonderful industry. The aesthetic breadth of independent publishers—whether they be nonprofit, for-profit, or university—is our best chance at resisting a monoculture of ideas and preserving a thriving ecosystem of thought in this country moving forward.

Those early decisions made by our founders—to see the South as a vital place made up of people who are worth listening to, a refusal to chase publishing trends and instead build a thoughtful institution that prizes mentorship, sustainability, and care—are the values of the Hub City Writers Project (and so many other small presses across the globe). That's the tradition we've been honored to carry forward here today.

To draw a clear line to the book you hold in your hands, that's how it works for us and I think it can work for other communities, as well. We were early proponents of a belief that now feels more urgent than ever: books build better communities.

I've witnessed how they can foster civic engagement, safeguard democracy, and serve as engines for empathy, transporting us into other people's frames of reference and helping us understand the world from perspectives beyond our own. I've seen how books helped restore Spartanburg's soul.

This collection is a celebration of that ethos and of the large and growing community who have made the work possible: the writers, editors, staff, booksellers, and readers who believe, as we do, that Southern literature is complex, expansive, and still unfolding.

And because you're holding this book right now, we're especially honored that the community includes you. Here's to thirty years and the chapters still to come. ⊙

M.R., August 2025

FORAGE

Carter Sickels

Not long after my grandfather died, my mother told me she had a dream about him. He was sitting on the edge of her bed with his big boots planted on the floor. He didn't speak. His presence was calm and comforting, like a nurse coming to check on her. He was so real, she insisted, he was right there. When my mother reached for him, her hand slid through empty space, shocking her awake. We were standing in the kitchen waiting for the coffee to brew when she told me about the dream. I must have been visiting her for some holiday or another. My mother didn't usually speak of her dreams or grief. That morning, her eyes were wet with tears. This was twenty-five years ago. I wondered if she'd been calling for him in her sleep. She missed him. I did too.

My husband and I read about the virus on our laptops and phones. We sit on the couch with our cat, Chloe, who at first seemed mildly curious or put out that we'd stopped leaving the apartment. Now, months later, she's adjusted to our constant presence. Today the number of dead in the US clocks at fifty thousand. Sometimes I read my mother's posts. She doesn't know how to make them private, or maybe she hopes I'll see them. They are mostly paranoid posts about liberals, links to bogus studies on the virus, and anti-masking memes. But today a scanned photograph of my grandfather looking up from his plaid recliner salutes me. My mother's caption says, *A real man.* I can't find any photos of me on her page, no matter how far back I scroll. For many years, it was just the two of us, and we were close, the way she was with her father. I was never close with my own. He lives somewhere in Texas.

My mother and I have not spoken in a decade.

My grandfather died in his sleep. Stretched out in his plaid recliner, an old Western running on TV, the local newspaper folded over his chest. The most natural way to go, people said, peaceful. An ordinary day of reading the paper and watching TV, and his heart just stopped. Alive, then not. We weren't prepared. This was twenty-five years ago. AIDS had killed tens of thousands, but I lived a sheltered life and had not yet lost anyone close to me. When my mother called to tell me my grandfather was dead, my knees buckled. I was twenty-five years old. I had just moved to New York, and I flew back to Cincinnati to help my mother arrange the funeral. She had lost her mother when she was young, and now she felt orphaned and lonely.

I haven't thought about my grandfather in a long time, but as I study the picture of him on my screen, the ache in my chest surprises me. I search through my closet and find more pictures in a cardboard cigar box. Pictures of him, pictures of my mother and me. A mix of the living and the dead. My husband sits next to me, looking over my shoulder as I leaf through the photos. Though it's the middle of the day, we're wearing robes and slippers, like old people. Chloe noses the box, then leaps off the couch, flaunting her lack of interest. There is a black-and-white picture of my grandfather as a young man, probably twenty years old, standing outside with a cigarette in his hand.

"He looks like you, or you look like him," my husband says. "Same smile. Same way of tilting your head."

But no, my grandfather was a big guy. Six foot three, heavyset. He possessed the appearance and attitude of a union worker who hoisted beams or cut sheet metal for a living. I rarely saw him wear anything but Dickies work pants, flannel shirts, boots with steel toes. Never blue jeans, never shorts. I never saw his bare legs, which I imagined to be as white as toadstools. Grandfather smelled like outdoors, like wind and dirt, like the first snow and a hint of liquor.

My grandfather did not cut sheet metal for a living. Before he retired, when I was a small child, he was a history teacher. My mother recalled him carrying a briefcase. Brown loafers with tassels. I've seen the proof in the photographs of him in a suit jacket and tie and ironed slacks, his black hair severely parted, like a stern but kind 1950s sitcom daddy. Very *Father Knows Best*.

I didn't know him as a suit man. He lived in town in a rambling Victorian with a deep front porch, but spent as much time as he could in what he called "the hills." Most days, he drove his rusty pickup out to a forest, I don't know which one, with his bird dog, Julie, an English setter. He fished in man-made lakes and cold creeks. He picked blackberries, which my mother baked into pies. My grandfather's massive hands and wrists were always laced with scratches, the evidence of briars and thorns he battled in the woods. He foraged for mushrooms, which he pan-fried in breadcrumbs and grease. I refused to even take a bite, despite his urging, turning up my naive nose. I also never went hunting or fishing with him, not like my cousins. I suppose this was because I was a girl.

I was not invited. I never witnessed my grandfather out in the wilderness, walking among the trees, crouched beside the strange and beautiful fungi shooting up from the muck.

Seventy-five thousand dead. Chloe, unbothered, stretches out in a spot of sunlight. My husband makes a mushroom soup and holds the ladle to my lips. "Try this," he says. I savor the rich, woodsy flavor, closing my eyes as if in ecstasy.

When my grandfather wasn't picking berries or fishing or hunting or foraging, we could find him stretched out in his plaid recliner, the same one in which he died, to read and watch TV. He read voraciously. The built-in bookcases in the cold back room held jars of pickles and tomatoes and green beans, and probably a hundred Louis L'Amour and Zane Grey paperbacks. He worked the crossword puzzle every morning, his fingertips stained gray with pencil lead and newspaper print. When we visited, he popped popcorn on the stovetop, drizzled on gobs of melted butter.

Now, like my grandfather, I like to wear flannel shirts. Like my grandfather, I feel at home with a book in my hands. I work crossword puzzles on an app on my phone. I eat mushrooms regularly, with delight.

When my mother told me about the dream she'd had of my grandfather, I was still her daughter. Now I'm a middle-aged man, and she cannot abide my splotchy beard, my receding hairline. When I came out to her, she said my grandfather was rolling over in his grave. You'll never be a real man, she said.

A few weeks ago, I signed up for an online mushroom identification class. On my computer screen, the mycologist waves from her spacious modern kitchen. She speaks effusively about the different kinds of mushrooms and holds them up to the camera, turning them this way and that, close-ups of caps and gills and stems.

I learn that mushrooms were a beloved food of the Roman Empire. Their root system, called mycelium, is multicellular. The mushrooms' network of microscopic fibers sprawls for miles underground, gathering strength to push up through whatever is covering them—forest floor, detritus, asphalt—to rise into visible structures we name and classify. Mushrooms feed on dead and decaying matter.

How did my grandfather, a history teacher in a suit, learn to pick mushrooms, to find the ones that were not poisonous, the ones that would nourish him? How did he learn to cook them? After he died, I asked my mother these questions, but she didn't know.

Oh, probably just from one of his friends, some old farmer, she said.

Maybe the farmer also taught him how to hunt birds. No, probably he learned this from his own father, a man I never met. Men teaching men to be men.

My grandfather liked to be alone in the woods with his bird dog. They flushed ruffed grouse—a sound he once tried to describe to me. He said the thunderous drumming of wings sounded like the heartbeat of God. For a moment, the birds rose, airborne and free. Then the crack of his gun. The retrieved, lifeless bird held so softly, gently in his beloved dog's mouth.

My husband, as a young man, attended funeral after funeral. He joined ACT UP protests, he lay down on the street while cops, some of them on horses, some of them making a statement by wearing latex gloves, beat and smashed bodies.

He shows me pictures of beautiful young men on his laptop. Chloe curls next to him and purrs.

"Tell me about them," I say.

I remember sitting at the dinner table at my grandfather's house, him serving the pan-fried mushrooms that I did not eat. I remember him as a kind, gentle man, the kind of man I wanted to be, but I had no way then to express this, I didn't have the words or understanding. I remember he said, All the queers should be sent to an island. Did my mother laugh? Did I?

My husband says such a conversation would not have been unusual. His parents said the same thing. They've changed their views. He talks to his mother almost everyday. They end the conversations with I love you. My husband is more forgiving than I am. He says it's not that. He says, "Life is short."

When my grandfather could no longer see the pages of his Westerns, my mother read to him, spinning myths and lies about heroic men on horseback.

The mushroom identification guide collects dust. The accumulation of missed moments twists and turns, reaching through the debris of our days. I already regret what I won't do. My husband says, Maybe you should call her. I'm afraid of hearing her voice. Afraid she will hang up.

I felt close to my grandfather, but I didn't know him, not really. My memories of him are nostalgic and comforting. Memories of his rugged, gentle masculinity. *A real man.*

My grandfather never met me as the man I am now. (Am I a man?) What would he say? Would he think I should be quarantined and exiled to an island? Would he, like my mother, tell me to go to a Christian therapist and get myself fixed? Or would he smile and shake my hand, man to man? Maybe he would take me with him into the woods. We'd lay down our guns. We'd crouch close to the earth, our hands searching for life.

My husband and I leave the apartment. We walk through the park and feel the warmth of the sun radiating on our faces. Grateful to be alive, to be healthy. On a stump, I spot strange orange fungi. "Probably poisonous," my husband says. "Won't kill you, but will make you sick."

My mother believes the virus is a government hoax. She said the mushrooms my grandfather fried tasted heavenly. I regret now that I didn't try them. He held out the plate to me, but I refused. They would have tasted crisp and meaty and buttery, as rich and real and giving as the earth.

Last night I dreamed of my mother. In the dream my mother, for the first time, called me by name. She touched my face. She said, You look like him. "She was sitting right here," I say to my husband. "I could have touched her. She was so real." ⊙

Cora Lee

Desiree Evans

Cora Lee turns fifteen today. She is not grown, although there are things about her that feel grown: the full shape of her tits, her thick hips, the rough voice that rumbles from her chest. She is an old woman trapped inside a younger girl's body, and she likes to think that maybe her oldness will come crawling out from inside of her one day soon, that by sixteen she will be weathered and gray haired, wise enough to know things about the world, like why praying makes the sleeping easier at night, and why no one seems worried about turning into dust one day.

Cora Lee turns fifteen today, but she is not too grown that she's forgotten how to laugh, swinging her wide-boned girl body through the hole-punched streets of the Ninth Ward. She understands the place she was born into is full of shadows. They slip into her open cracks, slide oozing into the gutters of her ribs, spill against the long, unbroken lines of her legs. These days she is all willow tree and bitter bark, and the shadows quake when she hiccups or laughs. So for now, Cora Lee moves with the shadows: She drinks instant coffee with a spoonful of honey from Baba Cool's farm, she wears yellow sweaters that are too long in the arms, and her soft flannel pajama bottoms drag in the dirt when she walks. On those nights when the world's gone slumbering, and the sky is a deep purple and the grass more blue than green, she finds a moment to listen to all she can: the moths bumping against the porch light, the crickets' chirps turning into night song, and the soft whispers whisking through the trees.

Cora Lee turns fifteen today, and she is sure the neighborhood folk will come to visit, will come to her with eyes wanting, needing, begging, and she will give to them something from inside her belly, a story maybe, a word of comfort, a cookie from her secret pantry of sweets. Because there are things she sees in others that remind her of the things she sees in herself, and there are evenings when folk are getting off work, after hours spent hidden in the dark kitchens of the quarters, hours spent cleaning and grinding and lifting. They will come walking her way, broke-down and bone-tired, and Cora Lee will put a hand to their shoulders and get offered back a thankful smile. There are days when Delma Willis will go crying down under the bridge because another of her girls has gone missing, and because Cora Lee hasn't yet figured out where girls get to when they go missing, all she can offer to do is hold the woman's hand and tell her about her missing brother, Jamal. And how Cora Lee used to walk down to the Dollar Tree just to see him riding by in his car, the sound of hip-hop curling out of his passenger-side window. She will always remember him as Lil Jay, walking bowlegged in his high-top Adidas, the shine of his one gold tooth when he smiled, and the quiet way he used to play jacks with her.

Cora Lee turns fifteen today, and that means summer will be coming fast and mercury soon, the heat like a wild, pulling thing, all golden-red skies and shirtless Black boys, and Tee Birdy's rumbling truck pulling into the front yard. Her memaw

Tee Birdy, who will shout too much when she sees Cora Lee. Tee Birdy, who will scare all the neighbors. At least that's what most folk say about her when there's something that needs saying about her. Tee Birdy shouts too much, or Tee Birdy cries too much, or Tee Birdy hollers like Jehovah done come down to save us all. But Cora Lee thinks the truth about this city is that it's not a place for a hollering woman anymore. Not since the storm. These days most people turn the hollering inside, and Cora Lee wonders if maybe that's why so many folk come to her looking like they done swallowed something sour, like the world is caught up deep inside their chests, like they're suffering from a cough that just won't expel itself. But Tee Birdy will yell when she needs to yell, and laugh when she feels there's something to be laughed at. She will throw her head back and open her mouth wider just to do it all a little louder, and she will watch Cora Lee out of the side of one eye, daring her to join along. Cora Lee knows there are other people in the world with this wildness in them, just like Tee Birdy. There are people that seem more oriented to the ways of the spirits than the ways of the living, people who pull in the sunlight and shimmer-shine with the glow of it. She thinks maybe her daddy was like that too, a vivid splash of color, something irresistible to the moonlight.

Today, Cora Lee is fifteen, and she sits on her porch swing so she can hear the wind moan through the old shotgun houses, and she thinks maybe being grown is gonna be a good thing, and she's already full with the feeling of it bubbling up inside of her. She thinks about her mama's burgundy dress fluttering on the clothesline, the way it gets caught in the breeze, full of the promises the wind brings. The way the sky always holds Tee Birdy's laughter, and how the fields of wildflowers hold the dreams of the missing.

Cora Lee pulls her brightest yellow sweater over her head, stretched tight around her curving, almost-woman hips. She climbs down the porch steps, and from one beat to the next, she takes off running through her yard. Running through the empty lots turned untamed jungle since the storm. Running past the rows of empty houses, and navigating the muddy paths and crumbling roads with familiar ease. She runs and runs and doesn't stop until she comes to the water's edge, the river's long grass and tangled weeds brushing against her aching calves. Her breathing comes hard, sharp; the pulsing heat of the day settles slick against her already-warm thighs. She drops to her knees and digs her hands into the soft, dark soil, the sticky-cool mud curling around her fingers. She imagines her hands weaving shadows back into the earth; she imagines planting herself into the ground, growing roots, growing stronger, growing older. Fifteen into fifty. One day into the next. She imagines herself a tree, and wonders if this is how the forest gets made. She could do this, she thinks. Sit here and soak in the rain and blossom in the light. Turn shadow into seed, turn girl into forest, turn holler into song. Cora Lee closes her eyes, breathes in the new day. Fifteen, and she thinks about the coming neighborhood folk, and the coming wisdom of age, and she knows that there are many things that will come to be understood by her in time. ⊙

French I

Ron Rash

Madame Lowery was the first French person we had ever known, though she wasn't from France. As she haughtily told us the first day of class, she'd been adopted by the French while an exchange student, something that high schoolers in Wisconsin, unlike here in the hinterlands of Carolina, had an opportunity to do. "Because of my Gallic sensibility and my impeccable command of their language, the host family concluded my soul was French," Madame Lowery announced, "and they are correct, which is why I shall eventually return there to live."

It was her first year of teaching, and how she chose to begin in rural western North Carolina I do not know. She was a last-minute hire when the teacher we'd expected, Monsieur Vickers, abruptly "retired" after allegedly fondling a mannequin at Wray's Department Store. Madame Lowery was probably twenty-one or twenty-two, but she appeared much older. Aside from her wedding ring, she wore long black skirts and a loose black jacket that hid what shapes lay beneath the white blouses she favored. Her black hair was always pulled back in a sumo-warrior bun.

She wore large, black-rimmed glasses and no makeup, which accentuated her paleness and intimated she spent weekends indoors, conjugating verbs and reading French newspapers. It was rumored that she did not shave her armpits. Madame Lowery's one acknowledgment that she was living in 1967 and not 1857 was a pair of stylish high heels, which made a loud tapping sound as she walked briskly down the hallway.

My French I section was first period. I and Mike Grier, my best friend and next-door neighbor, rushed in to claim back row seats. Other students soon came in and found their desks, last of all Henry "Meathead" King, who'd failed ninth grade twice and was awaiting a December birthday when, to the immense relief of the staff and faculty, he would drop out. Meathead, who'd given himself the moniker, sauntered in as the tardy bell rang, slumped into the seat closest to the door, and closed his eyes. Madame Lowery called the roll, then unfurled a map of France affixed above the blackboard. She tapped the map with a wooden pointer.

"Tomorrow I shall assign each of you a French name close to your English first name, and we will begin to express ourselves in the grandest of languages, but today, in English, we will discuss France and its people. France has made innumerable contributions to the world, and at the beginning of each class I shall, albeit briefly, mention a Frenchman or Frenchwoman behind these many accomplishments, particularly in the arts. But for now, let us begin by allowing you to name some of these contributions. Who would like to start?"

On the front row, Braxton Clodfelter's arm jerked upward as if controlled by a puppeteer.

"Oui?" Madame Lowery asked.

"The French invented the commode," the ninth grade's ultimate brownnoser volunteered.

"I would have hoped to have started with other achievements," Madame Lowery said, "but, oui, it is a French invention."

Missy Gaines raised her hand

"They built the Waffle Tower."

Madame Lowery grimaced.

"It is the *Eiffel* Tower, mademoiselle."

"French toast and French fries," Bobby Stuart said, keeping to the food motif.

"French kissing," Mike whispered to me, a bit too loud, causing Meathead King to open his eyes.

"French ticklers," Meathead said, a term many in the class did not know but Madame Lowery clearly did. She blushed, but strangely only her ears reddened. A French mannerism, I supposed.

"No more vulgarity," she said sternly.

Tugboat Thompson (Tugboat really was his first name. He'd once had to bring in a birth certificate to prove it), whose family owned the biggest chicken farm in the county, lifted his hand.

"They invented the guillotine," Tugboat offered. "They invented eating frogs too. My daddy raises chickens and he gets all tore up about that."

Madame Lowery placed a palm over her eyes and forehead, then, slowly, lowered the hand, opened her eyes, and sighed, seeing that she was indeed not on the Champs-Élysées but in Cleveland County, North Carolina.

"They eat frog *legs*," Madame Lowery said, "and I believe we should go ahead and open our textbooks and begin Leçon Un."

And from that moment on, I was doomed. In elementary and middle school I'd been labeled an "underachiever" and I did nothing to alter that label during high school, but even later, in college when I did try, I had no facility for foreign languages. All of which was confirmed when I made a 28 on our first test. *Roland*, a note in terse red handwriting said. *You made the second-lowest grade in the class. C'est inacceptable!*

But instead of trying harder, I did what I always did in my classes—sit on the back row and keep my mouth shut, hoping the teacher would leave me alone as I covertly read a book about something I was actually interested in. By osmosis I absorbed at least enough to pass a class, but not this time. My nine-week report card had three Cs, two Ds, and an F in French I. My parents half-heartedly threatened to ground me on weekends, but after years of meeting with school teachers and counselors I had worn them down. I can imagine them thinking, justifiably, that it was time to focus on my younger brother and sister to salvage the family's future.

Mike, however, after rivaling me with a 34 on his first test, had become quite studious. On the nine-week exam he made a respectable 83, raising his average to a C for the term. Because Mike had shown no similar interest in his other classes, one afternoon on the way home I asked why.

"Come with me and I'll show you why," Mike answered as we got off the bus.

His parents were both at work, so Mike led me into his parents' bedroom, opened the closet door, and after rummaging a bit, found what he was looking for.

We went to his room and he opened the *Playboy* and set it on his bureau.

"The French Chambermaid," the title proclaimed. Beneath the words, a stunning brunette wore a short black dress and white apron. A white cap topped her tightly gathered hair and a feather duster, held jauntily in her right hand, accentuated her provocatively tilted hips. "Ze room is not quite prepared for you, monsieur," a caption at the bottom declared.

The next two pages revealed that last preparations included the chambermaid shaking free her hair and stripping to a black bra and garter belt. On the next page even those had disappeared, and she sprawled naked on the bed. "You wish to enter now, oui?" the caption read.

"Hell yeah, oui," Mike said. "That's the way the women

are over there, buddy. You heard what Madame Lowery said about taking us to France this summer. If I know the language, well, that will give me an advantage. I mean, just look at her," Mike exclaimed, lifting the magazine for closer inspection. "I'd memorize a whole French dictionary for a chance to meet someone like that."

As I studied the photograph, I saw Mike's point.

"Oui," I said. "Maybe I'll start trying harder too."

But that night my relationship with Madame Lowery changed dramatically, in part because of the *Playboy.* By this point of my adolescence, I'd already had several of what Coach Beaks, my ninth-grade health teacher, called "nocturnal admissions." But as to what triggered them I only dimly recalled. This time, however, I remembered perfectly.

Madame Lowery sat not *at* her desk but *on* it, crossed legs dangling, loosed hair cascading down her back. She wore a chambermaid's black dress and apron. Her glasses were off and soon everything else too. Madame Lowery walked totally naked over to my seat, whose initial-carved top was no longer attached. She smiled, nodded at my lap, shifted her hips, and asked, "Oui, Roland?"

That was the end of the dream, but it was enough. The next morning, after wadding my underwear and putting them in the bottom of the clothes hamper, I got on the bus and headed to school. When I walked into Madame Lowery's classroom, she looked at me and frowned.

She knew, undoubtedly through the same telepathy that enabled teachers to discern which student was whispering as they faced the blackboard. This mystical power now exposed my depraved sexual fantasy to Madame. I might as well have thrown my gooey underwear on her desk and said "merci."

I stared at my desk the rest of the class, or almost the rest, because forty minutes in, Madame Lowery asked, first in

French and then in English, "Roland, are your thoughts on something besides French conjunctions?" A seemingly innocent question that my panicked brain interpreted as, *Roland, are you still thinking those disgusting thoughts about me?*

"No ma'am," I stammered. "I mean, madame. I'm not thinking about anything except conjoinings."

But Madame Lowery had turned her attention to Meathead, who was snoring not loudly, but noticeably. She wavered briefly but realized that a Meathead awake was more disruptive, so turned back to the blackboard. I lowered my eyes, not to gaze at the runic etchings of previous occupants but instead at my open textbook.

Because I was paying attention, just as I would for the next eight weeks. I studied every night. But no matter how hard I tried, mastering the language was like climbing the Alps wearing roller skates. When under stress, I had a propensity to mispronounce words, so language lab was especially hopeless. *Comme allez-vous, Roland,* Madame Lowery chided in my earphones, not *comma allah-view.* She asked me to try again and I heard an exasperated sigh, then a click signaling she was no longer listening. In early December when Madame Lowery handed back our last test grade, my average for the nine weeks came to 68. I had doubled my previous nine-week grade, which her note on the test acknowledged, *Your effort, Roland, while showing improvement, raises your mid-year grade only to 51, obviously not enough for you to pass. You must work even harder.*

But I believed I might yet avoid a mid-year F. The week before, perhaps in the spirit of Noel, Madame Lowery announced that the last class before Christmas break would be devoted to extra-credit projects related to France or its culture. Tugboat, who was also failing, and I shot up our hands. So did Missy Rollins, who was barely passing, and Braxton Clodfelter, who had an A but couldn't resist a few more brownie points.

I knew anything short of a full-scale replica of Chartres would *earn* me enough credit to pull me up to a D, but a project showing immense effort might convince Madame Lowery to raise my grade as an act of mercy, a word she knew well having corrected me repeatedly for pronouncing *merci* the same way. For two days, I pondered various ideas: hundreds of army men painted blue for France, brown and red for Prussia and England, to depict the Battle of Waterloo. But then I remembered the French were humiliated in that battle and Madame Lowery, like any good Francophile, might not wish to be reminded of that. I thought of catching a dozen frogs, cutting off enough legs for Madame and the rest of the class to have an appendage each as a French meal, but I'd always liked frogs, and besides, it was early December and they were hibernating.

It was when I saw my brother playing with his erector set that the perfect idea came to me. What better way to impress Madame Lowery than to recreate what she called the greatest symbol of French civilization, so I made a quick trade with my brother, his erector set for my ball glove. First, I polished each piece of metal with steel wool until it shone bright as a new dime. Then I set to work, using a photo torn from a *National Geographic*. To make my tower secure enough not to fall apart between home and Madame Lowery's classroom, I found an inch-thick piece of plywood for my foundation and half-inch wood screws to secure the baseplates, then secured the girders with the set's nuts and bolts. Up the tower rose, albeit slowly. I had as little aptitude for engineering as for French, and it took three afternoons and evenings to make the structure resemble the photograph. Once finished, it stood three-feet high.

My parents lauded my efforts, perhaps assuming that, if nothing else, their oldest child might get a job clerking in a toy store. But I wasn't through. The following day I spent my lunch period digging popsicle sticks out of garbage cans. I bought a sheaf of green construction paper, a bit of seeming luck since it was a school color, and I had my trees and foliage. Once home, I cut out triangles from construction paper, glued them to the popsicle sticks. Play-Dough rooted my trees to the plywood. I found two army men holding binoculars instead of guns and I had my tourists.

If I'd stopped there, all might have gone well, but as I mulled over my creation I remembered Madame Lowery saying that the Eiffel Tower could not be fully appreciated unless at night, so I went into the attic. Amid a jumble of Christmas decorations, I untangled two strands of white lights. I threaded them up from the base to the tin-foiled apex. By the time I finished, it was dark outside. I closed the bedroom door, shut off the overhead light, and plugged in the Christmas lights. They worked.

My sole concern after that was getting my project to school undamaged. I usually took the bus but my father agreed to drive me. We set the tower lengthways in the trunk and I gently gathered quilts around it. My father drove the two miles to the high school so slowly that cars lined up behind us as if in a funeral procession. Once there, I delicately raised the trunk. The tower was fine. I covered my creation with a bedsheet and took it straight to Madame Lowery's classroom.

"Posez-le là-bas, Roland," Madame said, pointing to the corner where something even bigger lay shrouded under a blue plastic tarp. I went on to my homeroom and waited impatiently for the first-period bell to ring.

When it did, I went back down the hallway to Madame Lowery's class. After taking attendance, she announced the order we would go in. I was last, and when my name was called Meathead turned and glared at me, clearly disgusted at my refusal to fail with dignity. Braxton stepped in front of the class with a brick-thick stack of notecards and droned on for twenty-five minutes about the sewers of Paris. Even Madame

Lowery's eyes had glazed over by the time he finished. Milly got up next with her own stack of notecards and discussed Marie Antoinette's unfortunate demise. The class was only fifty minutes long and I nervously watched the clock. Only twelve minutes were left for Tugboat and me. But Tugboat had no notecards. With uncharacteristic gravitas, he went to the corner and lifted the still-veiled project into his beefy arms. He politely asked Madame for the use of her desk and set down his burden. Tugboat lifted the blue tarp slowly, revealing a four-foot-tall double guillotine. It was an impressive sight, and I've always wondered what grade Tugboat got. I would have given him an A for the year. A wooden scaffold, two nylon fish stringers and a pair of hatchet heads loomed above a Barbie doll, a two-headed Barbie, because another slightly larger doll head with a grotesquely long neck was also attached between the shoulders. "La un premiere execution of la Siamese twins in human history," Tugboat announced solemnly, then donned a black ski mask he'd hidden under his shirt. It worked perfectly. When Tugboat let the fish stringers go, the hatchet heads whizzed down and severed both heads, causing the ketchup inside the plastic to ooze from neck and torso. Brenda Rollins put her hand over her mouth, gave a frantic look to get Madame's permission, and ran toward the bathroom. Madame Lowery looked nauseated as well but quickly composed herself

"Merci, Remorqueur," she said, checking the clock in hopes the bell was about to ring.

But I had eight minutes and so brought my project over to her desk, wiping away splattered ketchup with a Kleenex before setting down my edifice. I closed the blinds and, extension cord in hand, shut the door before cutting out the overhead lights. Only then did I take off the bedsheet. Believing words would dilute the full effect, I found the socket next to the door and plugged in the Christmas lights.

For a moment everyone seemed dazed. I stood and was about to announce "La Tower du Eiffel," but before I could, a voice came out of the dark, clearly Tugboat's.

"Lord a merci," Tugboat said, awe in his voice. "It's a big ole pecker."

And, to my horror, I saw that it did resemble a penis, tin-foil glans and all. Several girls screamed, another begging Madame to turn on the lights. But before anyone could move, Meathead King attempted his first full French sentence.

"Oui, Monsieur Tugboat," he said as the classroom lights came on. "Un penis magnifique pour le plaisir de Madame pendant les vacances."

Madame Lowery had not moved from beside her desk. Looking at her I suddenly understood a song lyric that had puzzled me for months. Madame Lowery *was* turning "a whiter shade of pale," so pale that it seemed she might disappear right before our eyes. Which I'm certain she dearly wished as Mike led a rising chant of *Oui Oui Oui*.

I stepped closer to the desk, arms crisscrossed overhead as if doing jumping jacks.

"Non, Non, Non," I countered frantically. "It's supposed to be the Eiffel Tower. I made it from my erection set."

That did it. Madame Lowery bolted from the classroom, high heels clicking rapidly down the hall. "Na pas penis, pas penis," I pleaded as I trailed her. I thought she was headed to the principal's office but she strode right past it, went out to the faculty parking lot, got in her Citreon, slammed the door, and drove off. Small-town gossip charted her progress for the rest of the day: apartment, utility company, bank, and a visit to the liquor store. By noon she was on I-85 headed east toward Charlotte, or perhaps Paris. I later imagined her driving the car right into the Atlantic, hoping it might float long enough to reach the safety of the French coast. So Madame Lowery had left behind the county and all of its inhabitants forever. Almost.

Though I stumbled through high school, I did get into a college where, despite D's in Spanish and Algebra, I graduated, after which I went to grad school in English before further astonishing everyone who knew me by becoming a writer. In perhaps the most ironic twist of all, when I was forty-eight my first novel was published in France, eliciting an invitation to a book festival in Vincennes. I was about to begin my session when a woman in a short, stylish black dress approached me. Her black hair was streaked with gray but her complexion was that of a much younger woman, one who appeared to spend little time out in the sun. It was this paleness that caused me to recognize her.

"Bonjour, Roland," she said, her smile a crescent of irony. "Ton français s'est-il amélioré depuis notre dernière entrevue?'"

For a few moments I racked my mind.

"Are you asking how long I've been in France?"

"No, Roland," she answered, raising a ringless hand to brush back a strand of hair, "but you have answered my question."

There seemed to be nothing else to say, but Madame Lowery did not turn to leave.

"Are you no longer married?" I asked to fill the silence.

"Why do you ask, Roland?" she said sardonically.

"Your hand," I blushed. "There's no ring."

"I was never married. The ring, like those hideous glasses, was merely a way to appear older, and less attractive." Madame Lowery paused. "Though perhaps I didn't hide it well enough in your case, Roland. I recall several times you looked at me with what appeared to be rather des yeux transis d'amour."

"It was the Eiffel Tower," I stammered. "That's all it was supposed to be, and I swear I was trying to say erect... erec*tor* set."

Madame Lowery shrugged, head tilting, palms turned upward in the Gallic manner.

"Well, anyway, Roland, you have done surprisingly well for

yourself, and in my way I am proud of you. I would even like to believe I made some small contribution to your success. You may remember that in class I spoke of Baudelaire and Giono, writers you greatly admire, or so the interview I read claimed."

As Madame Lowery paused, the event's host signaled it was almost time to begin the session.

"I guess I need to go," I said.

"I as well," Madame Lowery answered. "I fear I cannot stay for the session. Your accent recalls too many horrors."

She stepped forward and offered her cheeks for a kiss.

"I suppose we have both found our proper place in the world. Oui, Roland?"

"Oui, mademoiselle," I said, pursing my lips to avoid any drawl.

"Très bien, Roland," Madame Lowery said, and returned, soul and body, back to her place in the world. ⊙

The old man and the pool

John Lane

The old man appeared at the low chain-link fence and asked through the sparse yet blood-red blooming oleander, "Is this a public pool?" The old man wore swimming goggles and a red-striped towel wrapped around his hips and legs. He was tan and naked from the waist up. His platinum-gray mustache matched his curly hair. In a tinny voice like a wizard might use, he asked once again, "Is this a public pool?"

On Shearwater's patio encircling the pool, Trisha's best friend Joe focused instead on Faith, who had said for the second time that afternoon, "You need more pool loungers."

Joe sat on the pool's edge, his feet dangling in the water. He'd certainly heard the voice from the shrubbery, though he answered, "Enough with the frigging loungers, Faith. She knows."

"It's Thursday and we're leaving tomorrow," Portia chimed in from one of the royal-blue plastic loungers. She hadn't heard the old man. "And we're sitting around Trisha's pool counting loungers?"

"It's not actually Trisha's pool," Joe said. "It's one thirteenth her pool. What's that—the deep end of the pool?"

"Well, I'm glad I only own a one thirteenth share, because when Deep-End Pool Service comes to fix the filter later this afternoon it will be damn nice to divide the bill by thirteen," Trisha said. Fully reclined, she looked up at the Edisto sky. It was easy to understand why she didn't hear the voice calling from the blooming hedge. She imagined the clouds as cotton galleons sailing east to Seabrook Island. How many times that afternoon had she looked up and disappeared, staring away each time the conversation around the pool reached another absurd level of vacation banter?

In spite of her scrappy, single friends she always invited down, this was her peaceable kingdom, her Valhalla, her sanatorium for four weeks a year, one each season. Shearwater and the pool—that was where she and Larry had invested their first bundle in a share fourteen years earlier when Shearwater had been built, and it's what she requested from the divorce when her drinking was at its height. Larry gave in. He kept the Knoxville condo and she negotiated for the Edisto share. It took four years to kick the booze after the divorce, but she did, and since getting sober she'd enjoyed asking her four old college friends to join her—even Faith, whom she once was certain they would shun after they all left UT.

"What do you do when one of the other owners can't come and sells their week to a bunch of college kids and they trash the place? Who pays?" Travis asked. If he heard the old man, he, too, ignored him. He occupied the lounger next to Faith's.

"That's never happened," Trisha said.

"Why would a household of college kids ever end up on Edisto?" Joe deadpanned. "It's forty miles to the nearest vape shop."

"This is a family beach." Trisha was a little irritated. She stood up, retrieved the skimmer net, and dipped several shards of palmetto frond from the pool's surface. "That's why I like it here. The world falls apart around Edisto, but Edisto just keeps on keeping on."

"Having college kids around doesn't mean the world's fallen apart," Joe said. "It would be nice to go out to a big, loud bar and dance."

"Good god, Joe. Will you ever grow up?" Faith asked. "Your whole world is about you. You've got to be more sympathetic."

"I didn't suggest with college kids the world falls apart," Trisha said.

"It's what it sounded like," Joe said.

"Who put a briar up your butt, Joe?" Travis asked. "We're Trisha's guests. Chill out."

"It's a nice beach and I'm glad you invited us down for one of your weeks," Faith said, sipping from her Big Gulp cup with the bright-red straw. "And by the way, Joe, the lounger inventory would have mattered if Roxy and Lee had come over from Charleston."

"Roxy would have never gotten out of the pool," Joe said. "And Lee would have just stood around and pontificated."

"Stand up straight when you've got something important to say," Travis said, toasting the blue sky and their absent friend. "That's what he learned in public speaking."

"He's always been a pontificator," Faith said. "Didn't he major in English?"

"See what that got him twenty years down the line? The latest career move is selling Bitcoin."

"It's easy enough to get more," Trisha declared, putting the skimmer net down and sipping her Diet Coke. "We got these loungers from Costco."

"You need about twelve loungers," Faith answered, looking around the pool. "Travis, do you want another White Claw?"

"I need something stronger," Travis said, tipping his head back and removing his sunglasses. He smiled at Faith. "In the good old days it would be gin-and-tonic time."

"I don't care if you drink, Travis," Trisha said. "Just no glass at the pool." She glanced around the square of patio wedged between Shearwater and the dunes. Salt cedar, oleander, and sea oats framed the scene. As a teasing reminder of a much larger drama, she heard the surf slapping the sand shore just within earshot.

The old man had waited patiently as they jousted. Finally, he asked again, in the same tinny voice, "Is this a public pool?"

Everybody turned at once toward an opening in the oleanders. Could this be an apparition, like a shimmering mirage conjured from the summer heat settled over the island?

"No!" Trisha yelled when she located the source, surprised by the old man, the question, and the voracity of her own response. Before the old man came into focus Trisha had thought it might be her ex-husband Larry pulling a prank. Larry had not been at Shearwater in eight years. She immediately felt threatened by the voice pushing in from street side, at her own pool, with her old friends lounging around.

"You're obviously Week thirteen," Joe said to Trisha, standing up and walking closer to the shrubbery and squinting in the direction of the old man. "Unlucky thirteen—look at this. An old man in your oleander."

"I'm Week One, smart ass," Trisha said.

"Should we invite him in?" Joe asked.

"And offer him a drink? Get his opinion on how many loungers Trisha needs?" Travis countered.

"What good is it having a pool unless you can exclude people?" Joe asked.

Travis added, "You know, we'd be complicit if the old man had a stroke and drowned."

"We're not letting him in," Trisha said.

"Is he clean?" Joe asked.

"How could we possibly know if he is clean?" Faith asked.

"We could ask him to shower before he gets in," Joe joked.

"He's not getting in the pool," Trisha said.

"He's an old man," Travis said.

"I confess, he reminds me of Larry," Trisha said.

"He does look a little like Larry, now that you mention it," Faith said. "Same porn star mustache."

"If it's Larry, we should let him in to swim," Joe said.

"If it was Larry, we'd know," Travis said. "We all remember Larry. This isn't Larry. This is an old man in a muumuu."

"It's not a muumuu," Faith said. "It's a towel he's wrapped around his waist. It's more like a sarong."

Trisha shook her head. She certainly wasn't letting this old man in to swim, particularly when he had reminded her of her ex-husband.

Finally, the oleanders drifted back into place and the old man was gone.

"See what we've done?" Faith said, gazing down at the cerulean water. "We weren't very neighborly."

After the old man disappeared, the peanut lady's truck passed by on the side road. "I wonder if maybe the woman who drives the peanut truck knows anything about the old man?" Trisha asked. "I'll be back," she said and opened the gate.

"Cayenne, not plain," Joe shouted at Tricia.

"And make sure they're warm," Faith added.

Trisha had to speak louder than normal to be heard over calliope tune playing over and over. "Have you seen an old man in a sarong?" she asked the peanut lady through the truck's tiny window as the peanut lady handed over two bags of boiled peanuts.

"An old man in a thong?" the peanut lady asked.

Trisha laughed. "No, a colorful sarong. He was at our fence asking if this is a public pool."

"Did you let him swim?"

"No," Trisha said. "My friends got in an argument and he disappeared."

"You mean he vanished?"

"He was there one minute and gone the next."

"And you've never seen him before?"

"No, but at first I thought it was my ex-husband Larry."

"Do I remember Larry?" the peanut lady asked.

"He liked boiled peanuts, but we split up before your time here."

"He'll return," the woman said, sliding back into the driver's seat.

"How do you know?"

"It's a hot day and there aren't many pools around."

The afternoon seemed quite tame after the peanut lady drove away. If anyone thought any more of the old man as the afternoon deepened they didn't mention him. A vast ocean awaited just off the patio. Rafts of elegant pelicans floated past. Joe tried flinging a barb or two but the group ignored them. Even Faith seemed collegial, not mentioning the loungers. Trisha was preoccupied with her phone. She thumbed through hundreds of photos of the twenty-four weeks she'd spent with Larry at Shearwater. They'd been lucky. Larry managed property back in Knoxville he'd inherited from an uncle and could phone in instructions from anywhere. Trisha worked remotely doing accounting for a restaurant equipment company. Often their weeks at the beach were a combination of flurries of telecommunications and fun. Mostly, they'd kept the place to themselves. Their social lives consisted of the three bars on the island. That proved Trisha's undoing, as she drank more and more heavily through the years. Larry handled it better than Trisha, but the marriage fell apart anyway. Larry found ways to get to the bars without Trisha and sought comfort in a bartendress or two. Trisha never got over those transgressions and they helped ensure the settlement included the Edisto share, which made her happy.

And Larry? She wasn't really sure. They had no kids, and so there was nothing to keep them communicating. She'd run into him only a few times in Knoxville. Soon after the divorce, she started asking their friends down to Edisto. Only today had Larry's memory snuck back.

Later that afternoon, the old man reappeared and again he asked through the oleander, "Is this a public pool?"

Joe heard him first. "Go away," he said, swinging around. The old man didn't respond, but instead stood in the hedge smiling.

The others heard him, too, even Trisha, who dropped her phone. "This is my pool," she said with urgency in her voice.

The old man waited and watched.

"Could he be deaf?" Travis asked.

"He's screwing with us," Joe said. "Maybe he's a little off."

"I think his question is totally serious," Faith said. "He wants to know if this is a public pool."

"It's not public," Trisha said. "It's private."

"Doesn't seem very private to me," Joe said, smirking. "This old man keeps showing up and poking his head in."

Right then the woman from the Deep-End Pool Service pulled up at the fence in her panel van. She approached the lounging friends and raised her hand in greeting. "What's the problem with the pool?" she asked.

"It won't circulate," Trisha explained.

"Could be a dead frog," the pool woman said. "Could be something worse."

"What could be worse than a dead frog?" Joe asked.

"Condenser," the pool woman said. "If it's a condenser it could take a week to get the parts."

The pool woman put down her bag of tools. She had bleached, surfer hair and was dressed in flip-flops, shorts, and a Hawaiian shirt. She went right to work, leaned over and tripped the switch on the system to off.

"Who's the old man?" she asked, glancing toward the oleander.

"He wants to know if it's a public pool," Trisha said.

"Well, if it is a public pool, then I'm at the wrong house," the pool woman joked. "Are you letting him in? He's hot."

"You mean overheated, or sexy?" Joe asked.

"Overheated," the pool woman said. "It's a hot day. That's why he wants to swim."

"What should we do?" Travis asked.

"You mean about the condenser, or the old man?"

"We're not doing anything about the old man," Trisha said. "He'll go away if we ignore him. He did before."

The pool woman jiggled out a pipe and out fell a wilted ten-inch snake. "Here's your problem," she said. They all stood over the snake and looked down.

"That's a big dead worm," Joe said.

"It's a decomposing water snake," the pool woman explained. "The system should kick on when I hit the switch."

"Are you going to leave it on the grass?" Trisha asked. "It smells."

"I think it's pickled in chlorine," Travis said.

"Get me a garbage bag and I'll haul it away."

"We still have the problem of the old man," Faith said. "I think we need to let him in. He could be somebody's father."

"There's no way he's coming in," Trisha said.

The pool woman flipped the switch and listened as the system began filtering water again. "You're good to go."

"Look, he's gone," Joe said. "It's a private pool again."

The next morning Trisha slipped out early and made coffee for those still asleep. They'd all agreed to all be up for sunrise. As the first light rose, she wandered onto the deck and looked out at the horizon turning pink and took a picture as she always did. All she could think about was Larry, and how he loved the early morning out on the porch. Her eyes drifted down and she saw in the rising light the old man's colorful towel piled in a heap in a lounge chair. She didn't see the old man. Where was he?

She looked back into the house and saw Shearwater lit up where they had left some lights on. Was no one else awake yet? Was the old man swimming this early? Could he be below, in the pool? She had an awful feeling. What if the old man was floating face down in her pool? Was she losing her mind? Was she the sort of person to find an old man dead in her pool? A gilded array of clouds lit up with the sunrise, but Trisha wasn't interested anymore. What if the old man was dead in the pool? Their day would go downhill in a hurry.

Just then Portia came up behind Trisha with her coffee and looked down and saw the old man's towel and screeched. They both inched forward on the deck and looked down. The old man was there, collapsed on the edge of the pool, splayed out, face down. He wore black Speedos.

"Speedos on an old man. I didn't have to see that. Somebody needs to go down and see if he's dead," Joe said, coming up behind them to look down. He sipped calmly from his mug.

"Joe, shut the hell up. This isn't funny," Faith said.

Travis came out on the porch with his coffee. "What's everybody looking at?" he asked.

"It's the old man," Portia said. "Down there."

Travis saw where they were all looking, dropped his coffee immediately and sped down the steps. Soon he was cradling the old man and tugging him onto his back. Then Travis began CPR.

"Is he okay?" Faith yelled down at Travis.

Travis didn't answer, halfway through the procedure.

"Call 911," Travis finally yelled between resuscitations.

"Joe, you call," Portia said.

"No, you call," Joe countered.

"Joe, call the damn EMS," Faith said, exasperated.

"No, matter who calls, we're all up shit creek," Joe said. "I've got things to do today and I don't have time for a bunch of questioning."

"We're on Edisto and the EMS department is small. It won't take long," Trisha said.

"Oh yeah, so you think. If he's dead we might be here hours," Joe continued. "Or days."

"We can't be here days," Trisha says. "Week Two is due in tomorrow."

"He's coming around!" Travis yelled from below.

They all rushed down the steps and gathered around the old man who was indeed conscious.

Trisha was relieved to see him stirring. "You know, this is the first time since we saw this old man that I've quit thinking about Larry," she said.

The old man's eyes opened. He looked at each face in the welcoming circle above him and asked, "Is this a public pool?" ⊙

The chairs in your parlor

Kelsey Ronan

All that summer, across Indiana to Chicagoland, Brianna played Vivaldi and Pachelbel, Taylor Swift and Etta James, in churches, country clubs, rustic barns, microbreweries, and hotel banquet halls. She was the only undergrad in the string quartet, offered the gig after the cellist left on a Fulbright Scholarship to Argentina. She rotated two black maxi dresses, shivering in the air-conditioning or sweat rivering from her bra to band to the small or her back. She took off her strappy sandals as soon as the quartet buckled into Dagyeom the viola's SUV. They split the money and the occasional catering spoils, stacked their cases and stands in the trunk. Harper and Grace, the violins, sat in the back and guffawed at the Instagram stories of people in their cohort, complained about the demands of their TA positions, the dumb undergrads. Brianna sat upfront with Dagyeom. She watched for the blinking lights of the wind turbines to approach, their blades churning the dark. It meant the drive would soon be over, that they'd be back to Dagyeom's place in the neighborhood where all the grad students lived, too, on a street of shabby Victorian houses divvied up into apartments, bikes chained to the porch rails. Brianna's car waited in front of Dagyeom's place. He never said goodnight, but waved over his shoulder, mounting the porch steps. She drove herself home across the quiet city and over the river toward campus, to the blocky apartment complexes where she and all the other undergrads lived. All over town, the bar lights and fast-food neon burning, but the sidewalks empty. The elevator and the hallways of her building quiet. As a kid, Brianna fantasized about being locked into a department store after closing—she'd wait in a bathroom stall with her knees pulled up to her chest or crawl under a display bed heaped in creamy linens and pillows. She imagined it felt something like this. The music still twitching in her fingers. The thrill of getting away with something. The illusion that everything around her was hers and it was all free because there was no one there to demand payment. She imagined texting Dagyeom—*you still up?*—and they'd meet, the empty town to themselves, and say all the things they never said in his car. It was the summer between her junior and senior year, and the first that she hadn't gone home.

This weekend, though, the first broiling weekend of July, Brianna is missing Saturday's gig in Crawfordsville because, after she resisted the first two guilt-laden calls, her mother texted, *We need to talk about this in person but this is probably Nanas last fest and youll regret it if you dont come and Im gonna have a real hard time forgiving you.* Brianna first felt relieved that she was no longer trapped in her mother's melodrama. She could surely call her grandmother and congratulate her on her retirement from the Elvis fan club, she thought; it wasn't this big a deal when she retired from her job last year. *I didnt raise you to be selfish,* her mother texted after Brianna said she had to work. And maybe she could read Brianna's next untexted thought—*you didn't raise me at all*—and so, in a pang of guilt, she offered cash. *If you need the gas money just say so I'll venmo it.* Brianna had an idea.

At the state line, Brianna's GPS welcomes her to Michigan. The expressway becomes a lunar landscape, the blacktop cratered with potholes. The billboards stop screaming about abortion and Jesus and fireworks. Now there are alternating ads for cannabis dispensaries and Pure Michigan campaigns of Great Lakes shoreline and lighthouses. Indiana wanted you to fear God and celebrate America. Michigan wanted you to get your toes in the sand and get blown out.

Construction slows traffic to a single lane outside Monroe then stops all together when Brianna reaches Detroit's outer burbs. It's rush hour. She checks her phone too often. She's hungry and trying to ignore it. She will spend tonight and tomorrow at the state fairgrounds for the 25th Annual Michigan ElvisFest in the bosom of her white-trash matriarchy and then she'll just make it to the Sunday gig. Her cello lays across the back seat. She reads every billboard inviting her to stop in for a free first-time-customer pre-roll or edible, curbside and delivery available. The sun beats her windshield and her car says it's 105, which can't be right, but she has to keep turning up the air-conditioning, and she's anxious about all the gas she's burning, all that money evaporating into nothing.

It takes Brianna a moment, past the ticket table and the flea market, to locate her mother and grandmother on the fairgrounds. The perimeter of the Michigan ElvisFest is marked by a semicircle of food trucks and merch stands; beyond them a line of RVs. On stage, a teenage boy is leaning into the microphone, his hair whipped into a black pompadour, his shoulders squared by a black-and-pink sport jacket. The air is heavy and his baby-fat cheeks gleam with sweat. *They said you was high-classed / Well, that was just a lie.* The fairground is dotted with camp chairs and picnic blankets. Brianna's mother and grandmother are under a tree, left of the stage, propping their feet on a cooler serving as a makeshift ottoman. As Brianna nears, her mother stands and waves with both hands like she's on the side of the road, flagging down help.

Her grandmother has stopped dyeing her hair. For all of Brianna's memory she's worn it blonde, parted it in the middle and secured in a braid she could easily pin up inside the cap she wore in the cafeteria of the private school where she worked, ladling pasta and gluten-free alternatives for the children of automotive executives, professional athletes, lawyers, and surgeons. When her arms were sore, she asked Brianna to drag the plastic tip of Revlon Colorsilk in Ultra Light Natural Blonde over her pink scalp. It was because her grandmother was staff that Brianna could attend the school in the first place. The tuition waived because the lunch lady was her legal guardian.

Her mother embraces her, a crush of sweaty breasts and the synthetic floral of her perfume. "Thank you," she says into Brianna's hair. Brianna leans down to kiss her grandmother. On the ample chests of both women is the eternally youthful, slightly melancholy face of Elvis Presley. Her mother is wearing star-shaped earrings and shimmery purple eyeshadow. On her grandmother's shirt, Elvis' face looms over the image of Graceland, a souvenir from a trip to Memphis they took before Brianna's mother was released. *Welcome To My World,* the shirt says.

The boy on stage is stretching into the big crescendo end of "Now or Never." He hasn't earned his following yet, and the space in front of the stage is empty, the festivalgoers in their chairs and milling between the food trucks, but a polite, encouraging applause ripples over the field.

Brianna tells them about the terrible traffic, excusing her

lateness. She'd missed the national anthem and the introductory remarks from Janice, the president of the Elvis Fan Club. She'd missed the special thank-you to her Nana, but it was always the same. "Let's all give a big hand to Betty, our incredible event coordinator and founding member of the Michigan Elvis Fan Club." Through her childhood and beyond, Brianna had helped her grandmother fold newsletters and ElvisFest announcements into envelopes, nauseated from the bitter adhesive. Brianna hadn't had to hate the fest because in all Elvis spaces, like Walmarts and thrift stores and the bars downriver where Nana went to see Elvis tribute artists through the year, she never worried about running into anyone from school.

Her grandmother asks, "You eat yet, sweetie? Your mother made egg-salad sandwiches."

"Too hot to eat," she lies. Among other things Brianna is trying to change about herself, she is trying to lose weight. "The turnout looks good this year, Nana."

"We need to eat them before the mayonnaise goes bad. We're going to have the peanut butter and banana tomorrow for the vigil, so we should finish the egg salad today, we don't want to take them back home."

"Mom, they're in the cooler, it's fine." Brianna's mother gives her a pained smile. Brianna asks what she's missed. There's a chair for her but she sits on the grass, stretching her legs cramped from the drive, smoothing her skirt over her thighs. No one seems to hear her question, or maybe because ElvisFest is largely the same every year, no one feels compelled to answer.

"I just don't trust mayonnaise out in heat like this, Mel. Salmonella."

"*Okay*, Mom. Bri, baby, why don't you sit in a chair? We also have those Little Debbie cakes you always liked. Remember when you were little and you'd pick off the frosting and eat it first?"

"The ones you get at Christmas, shaped like trees," her grandmother said.

"The little green sprinkles all over the goddamn floor," her mother said.

"You used to drive your mother crazy." Her grandmother cackles until she starts to cough.

"Mom," Brianna's mother says.

"Betty!" someone says, and a woman in leggings and a Hawaiian shirt with Elvis' face repeating amongst the frangipani blooms is sweeping in for a hug. "I heard you're retiring and now I know that can't be right."

The woman starts to exclaim about her Nana's weight loss, and Brianna takes advantage of the distraction to immerse herself in her phone, as she has wanted to do for hours. She pulls open the quartet's group text. The violins, Harper and Grace, are pissed at her for giving just a week's notice that she'd be missing tomorrow's gig. She'd lied and said her grandmother was in the hospital. But it was hard to find a cello in the summer, impossible on such short notice, and when they did find a friend of a friend, it was a player from the Indianapolis Symphony Orchestra who insisted on a rate that meant they'd each have to forfeit a bit of their usual cut. Brianna had apologized profusely. Dagyeom, though, seemed unbothered. She texts him now to see if he wants anything from Detroit. Or rather, she composes parts of sentences she then deletes, straining for something quippy, something that both gives nostalgic reverence to their hometown and teases it.

So you want me to bring you back a Faygo or something?

What's your Faygo of choice—Rock & Rye or Moon Mist?

She tries both all lowercase, with punctuation and without, and deletes.

When Brianna auditioned for the quartet, sure these grad students would never let her in, she told them she was from

Detroit originally. Dagyeom had cut in. "Okay, but are you *actually* from Detroit?"

She recognized this tone. "East side," she said. "Mack and Alter." She felt she was owed this. She was only lying by a couple blocks and she was a fraud anyway in Grosse Pointe.

He wasn't from the city proper either: He said Madison Heights, but maybe he was really from Troy and his dad was an engineer or something. She'd earned his begrudging respect.

For all of May, through the first weekends of wedding season, Dagyeom's quiet felt personal. An old sense of inadequacy, unfeminist and boring, stirred within her. She thought she had exorcized the misogyny she'd internalized, healed it with body positivity and a respectable number of sexual partners who maybe weren't hot but were all smart and respectful. But with Dagyeom, she considered her size 14 clearance dress among the delicate brides and bridesmaids of the Midwest—French-manicured fingers pressing away tears from heavily lashed eyes, flower crowns and tiaras in their hair—and she thought she gloomily understood why he never asked her if she wanted to take up the aux cord or if the AC was up high enough.

Then in June, she had a glimmer of hope after packing up in a rustic barn festooned with fairy lights in Fort Wayne. They'd spent a ceremony behind a maid of honor in a mermaid dress with the kind of ass you usually see on pop stars and women who shill makeup and fitness content on social media. Her bare shoulders were bronzed and shimmery.

From the back seat, Harper leaned forward and said, "Hey Dag, I saw you checking out the, ahem, cake." Grace snickered.

He rolled his eyes and turned the key in the ignition. "Yeah I love a girl spray-painted brown and covered in sparkles."

The acid derision in his tone flooded her with hope. He had said what he didn't like, and she was not that kind of girl.

When Brianna's roommate was out, she listened to the

Leonard Cohen and Lou Reed songs from his playlists in the bathtub and thought about the smell of his suit jacket that time he'd wiggled out of it at a red light and handed it to her: the swift waft of sweat and cologne as she'd folded it. The narrow angles of his hips and shoulders. She knew after defending his thesis in the spring he was going to backpack across Europe. Vienna, Berlin, Budapest, Krakow. He'd busk on the Charles Bridge in Prague. One night on the drive back from Muncie, she said she'd never been to Europe, straining past her awkwardness to her working-class Detroit cred. He said she totally should. He made a nonchalant aside about how she could join him if she wanted to. Even with poor-kid financial aid and a series of work-study jobs, she had $30,000 in student loans and still her senior year ahead. She was supposed to be living constantly in first-generation gratitude and determination. Her grandmother hadn't given her a silver spoon, but something heavier: fancy things she had to work to keep. She had no business thinking about Europe. Still, for weeks she'd thought of little else.

Another Elvis gyrates and sneers on stage. The fairgrounds smell like onion rings and barbecue. It inspires her.

She types, *Hey might hit up a coney on the drive back tomorrow. Want anything?*

She hits send.

Brianna makes it through an up-and-coming Elvis tribute artist from Ohio who messes up the lyrics to "Shake Rattle and Roll." The first night headliner, Robert Washington, who bills himself as the Black Elvis and whose merch table is stocked with shirts that say Black Elvis Matters, is coming on at nine, and she'd like to make her first two runs before then. In line for the Porta Potty, she consults her map, opens the tabs on her browser to confirm. Dagyeom has not responded and she assures herself this is because he is at rehearsal, or deep in thought, listening to *The Academy in Peril* in his chunky headphones, and not because she has said something stupid. She congratulates herself on dodging the egg salad, the accomplished emptiness of her stomach.

"I'm worn out from the drive," Brianna tells her grandmother. Her mother's gone to the beer tent. "I'm just gonna take a little nap in the car."

Her grandmother's face is soft and luminous with the heat. "You feeling okay, honey? You just got here."

She tells her grandmother she just needs a few minutes. Her grandmother smiles at her.

Brianna gets behind the wheel, pulls out of the fairgrounds, and follows the GPS's directions to the first dispensary. Before she left Indiana she'd compared shops, calculated sales and first-time-buyer perks and discounts so that she was buying the smartest thing at each place, made a map. Everything is paid for; all she has to do is pull up and show her ID. There was no limit to how much you could buy in a day, but you were limited by law to 2.5 ounces per transaction.

The few times she'd smoked weed it had made her anxious and hungry, but as she prepared for this trip, it had been nice reading the descriptions of the various pleasant things they'd do to you. *This odoriferous flower offers a profile of crisp citrus, sweet earth, and wildflowers. Its strong physical effects and uplifting mental high make it a nice match for folks contending with restlessness and pain.*

She liked the lyric psychedelia of their names. Ghost Train Haze. Dark Rainbow. Private Banana. It reminded her of a trip to Sephora with the girls she went to school with. All the lipsticks with their salacious names. "This one's called Orgasm," Collette read, a knowing smirk. They gasped when Bri put the tester of a lip gloss up to her actual mouth. "The *germs*," Maeve said. "You're supposed to test it on your *hand*."

"You probably have like a million diseases now," Collette said.

"You might be pregnant, too," Delaney said. Brianna stood in Sephora with her face on fire and her hands empty, no money to buy the yoga pants and bras they put on their mothers' cards.

Now, Brianna pulls into the curbside delivery slot and rolls down her window into a skunky waft. A guy in a lanyard comes out for the Michigan ID that verifies that, as of three months ago, she is twenty-one. He swipes it. He hands her a paper sack with the receipt stapling it shut and tells her to have a good one. She repeats the process at two more dispensaries. Then her mother calls.

"Where the hell are you?" In the background, another Elvis bellows about his broken heart and his aging fans holler.

"Just super tired. Give me just ten more minutes."

"Do you need to go home? You're worrying Nana."

"Ten more minutes."

Her mother sighs but she hangs up. When Brianna finds the women of her family back at the fairgrounds, Robert Washington, in a bedazzled and caped white jumpsuit, is thrusting to "Polk Salad Annie," a song about a poor girl whose mother is on the chain gang, who picks wild greens for her family's dinner. Her grandmother is standing up at her camp chair, clapping along, her mother beside her. She hasn't had the energy to go up to the stage yet today. She's saving herself for Leo Days, she said. When they raise their arms, Brianna sees the sweat of their pits, under their breasts. "You're no fun, baby," her mother yells over the music at her.

When Brianna's mother got out of prison, she moved in with Brianna and her grandmother in a two-bedroom apartment where Detroit's east side ends and suburban affluence begins.

Brianna could look at Detroit from her bedroom window. She could throw something at Detroit, if she wanted to.

The view from the window is unchanged but Brianna's bedroom is long gone. The walls are now purple and her high school graduation photo is framed on the dresser beside the clutter of her mother's makeup and jewelry. In plastic shelving units and totes are the collections of occasional, generally abandoned hobbies: a sewing machine and piles of fabric, wire and jars of beads, supplies for making soy candles. Essential oils from a failed attempt at self-employment. Brianna once felt guilty for taking the room while her mother and grandmother shared the larger room with a screen partition between their beds, or slept in shifts when her mother was working the overnight shifts at gas stations and coney islands. Now when she is home her mother insists on sleeping on the couch so that she can have the bedroom back.

Her mother and grandmother are stingy with the air conditioner, mindful of their electric bill. A ceiling fan pushes the heavy air around and through the open window there is a drone of cicadas.

Brianna lays her cello case out on the floor and kneels to unzip it. Nestled along the instrument are the bags she's procured so far, and she takes out each, upending it and lining her inventory over the rug. The smell is intense. There are zippered bags of edibles and flowers, and pre-rolls in tubes that remind her of tampon applicators, but are brightly colored, labeled in graffiti fonts and cartoons. Most places gave first-time customers a free pre-roll or package of edibles, so even though the taxes were higher than she thought, she's pleased with what she's gathered and what she has left of her savings.

Brianna treats herself to one gummy. Pops it into her mouth and works it between her teeth. It tastes like dirt and corn syrup. She can taste it still after she brushes her teeth.

After ElvisFest, Brianna would spend the summer at dozens more weddings, most of them in Indiana, where there were no dispensaries because cannabis hadn't been legalized. She would encounter thousands of guests and caterers, facilities staff, groomsmen who hung around the back door talking about hungover they already were and how fucked up they were going to get. Mark up the prices, turn a profit. By the end of the summer she'd have so much money she could go to Vienna and meet up with Dagyeom.

She thinks about that while she tries to get comfortable, shifting atop the sheets, waiting for the drug to activate. She draws the spires of important buildings in imagined skies, moody gray and heavy with history. When she was younger she would think about the homes of the girls at school who invited her over for birthday parties. They had whole rooms she didn't: foyers and sunrooms and parlors. Rooms unlike this one, where, on the other side of the wall her grandmother keeps coughing and coughing and clearing her throat.

Saturday afternoon, Brianna, a trickle of low-fat vanilla cream from her cherry Dilly Bar from the Dairy Queen stand melting down her forearm, watches a man decades older than Elvis Presley lived to be thrusting in a spangled jumpsuit to "Suspicious Minds." It had been torture getting back to the fairgrounds. She fell asleep before the edible kicked in, but then she couldn't wake up. She'd been asleep for twelve hours when her mother let herself into the bedroom. "Bri," she said. "We're gonna be late." Brianna was hungry and slightly dazed. By the time she was out of the shower her grandmother was stuffing the peanut butter and banana sandwiches into their Ziploc bags and it was time to go.

Her neighborhood looked unbearable in this particular

daylight. The landscaping vans made their usual rounds. There was the buzz of weed wackers and the shrill calls of small children watched over by women in expensive athleisure wear. Her mother and grandmother in fresh Elvis tees. Her mother tipped the cooler on the lawn, yesterday's melted ice running into the grass. "Shit," she said, when the water splashed her sandals, over her painted toes.

Her mother said it was pointless for Brianna to drive separately, so Brianna said she'd drive them instead.

This her mother would not accept. "You can't drive. You just got up."

"Is that like a law now?"

"You and your lead foot make your grandmother nervous. We don't need you driving us half-asleep and speeding like a lunatic."

"I'm wide awake. I'm a good driver."

"The chairs are already packed."

Brianna submitted, a flare of panic in her stomach. From the back seat, the city she pretended to be from rose up around the car, then receded into bland suburb again. Her grandmother put in a CD of Elvis gospel and kept making a noise like she was trying to swallow something lodged in the back of her throat.

"When you think of all the people who went to jail for that shit," her mother says as they drive beneath the umpteenth cannabis billboard. She is talking about herself. Her grandmother punches the buttons of the stereo, skipping past "I'm Gonna Walk Dem Golden Stairs." *When I die, when I die.*

It was still new to Brianna that certain facts of her life could be lifted up, details slightly tweaked. She considers the grad school application essays she'll write after she gets back from Europe, if she does come back. Her hardscrabble life in Detroit. Raised on Elvis by her lunch-lady grandmother while her mother tried to pull herself up by her bootstraps. Elvis's father went to prison, her grandmother used to tell her; he forged a check after a man shorted him on the sale of a pig, and look at all Elvis accomplished, a musician like her, after all.

On the fairgrounds, three camp chairs, a cooler sloshing today's melting ice, and a bag with sunscreen and bug spray. Her grandmother's purse rattles with pills when she rummages inside it. She is quieter today. A woman in a *Birthday Girl* sash and big sunglasses swings her hips at the front of the stage, surrounded by friends. Their gel manicures shine on foam beer koozies. A group of people from assisted living dance in a circle.

"You should be up there," her mother says. "Mom, remember that Christmas she came home and played 'Can't Help Falling In Love' for us?"

"Don't get me started, Mel."

Brianna played that one a few weekends ago at a wedding in Muncie. The bride was a widow, middle-aged and weepy, and the groom's sons were his best men. Brianna thought of telling Dagyeom about herself on the drive home, after Harper protested Steve Reich's "Cello Counterpoint" until he turned it off. She used to do that sometimes when she was little, when she was in the car with her grandmother, returning from prison visits, and her head felt too full of noise for the oldies station. It seemed better, though, to bat this memory away. She wanted to propel herself farther and farther away from herself, toward this new person she was going to become.

Her grandmother unfolds a blanket she'd bought in the Elvis market, admiring it again. Brianna had been there twice already, circling the vintage Graceland souvenirs and gold plastic aviator sunglasses with fuzzy black sideburns flopping from the arms, for the air-conditioning. Her grandmother had insisted on buying her a key chain. Elvis pouting under the youthful flip of his pompadour.

Brianna forces a yawn. "I'm going to go take a nap in the car," she says. "Can I get the keys, Mom?"

Her mother sighs, agitated. "It's hot as hell and you're going to sleep in the car?"

"I just want to lie down for a minute."

Her grandma's cool hand flutters up to her forehead. "You feel fine."

"I'm not sick, Nana, just tired."

"You're twenty-one years old. Why the hell do you need a nap?"

"Mel, she works hard and she had a long drive yesterday."

"She's got some guy she wants to talk to, I'd bet dollars to doughnuts." She looks to Brianna. "I see you on that phone all the damn time."

But the keys drop into Brianna's hand. She offers to take the Elvis blanket for her grandmother. She feels her mother's skeptical gaze on her as she strides toward the exit.

In the parking lot of each dispensary she shoves her new bag of merchandise under the folded Elvis blanket. On the way back to the fairgrounds, the low-fuel warning comes on. Her mother always let the gas tank drain to the last miles before she stopped for gas. Brianna stops at a gas station to put in a gallon. The needle inches. Her phone buzzes with another text, her mother asking her where she is. Brianna is annoyed. She had enough gas in her own car. Still, there was enough left in her bank account to buy gas on the drive from ElvisFest to the gig, to buy something for Dagyeom if he answered her text. She is impatient for the hours to pass, for the state welcome sign to appear with its red boot, for the firework billboards, the fleeting miles back to her new life.

As the sun sets, just before the candlelight vigil concludes this year's festival, Flint-boy Leo Days, darling of the Michigan

Elvis Fan Club, does sexy-rebel fifties Elvis. He sweats through "All Shook Up" and "Shake, Rattle, and Roll." He rolls up to the tips of his toes. He windmills his arms. He's down on his knees crooning "Are You Lonesome Tonight?" to the women standing in front of the stage, her grandmother finally among them. Brianna's there, too, hanging back, arms folded over her chest, shifting her weight. Her mother sings along, sweating off her makeup.

Do the chairs in your parlor seem empty and bare?

Do you gaze at your doorstep and picture me there?

The song ends. Leo Days reaches out a hand to Brianna's grandmother and invites her on the stage. Then Nana is there, in the stage lights, in front of the backing band, and a man pretending to be Elvis is thanking her for her years of service to the memory of Elvis Presley and all she has done to champion musicians like himself. People on lawn chairs clap. Some people put down their coney dogs and barbecue plates to clap too. Her grandmother in her *Jailhouse Rock* tee is dabbing at her face with a disintegrating ball of tissue. Elvis's arm is around her. "Your Elvis family is always here for you," he says. "There may be dark days ahead, but call on us anytime day or night. We love you so much." And Brianna wonders if that's a strange thing to say at a retirement party. On her last day at the cafeteria, the school just sent her home with flowers and a card they made kids sign.

Brianna's mother is sobbing beside her. She usually doesn't cry until the candlelight vigil, when all the Elvises come onto the stage for a grand finale honoring the life and legacy of Elvis. Maybe she'd had too much to drink in this heat. She claps and whoops. "That's right, Mom!" she hollers. "Love you!" she cries. She presses away tears then she reaches back for Brianna's hand, pulling her closer. The lights illuminate her face, the smeared eyeliner and glitter flakes. Leo Days, closest any of them will get to the King, dedicates "You'll Never Walk Alone" to Betty. Her mother's hand is a hot trap and she wants to pull it free.

Brianna loads the camp chairs and the cooler into the trunk. She thinks she can smell it, but the spike of anxiety hits her. The smell has escaped the dozens of plastic packages. The cannabis has marinated in the heat of the interior of her mother's car, which now smells like pure drugs.

"The fuck?" her mother says as soon as the door is shut.

In the backseat, Brianna says nothing. She needs something to look at, so she looks at her phone, opens apps at random. Her period is another week away, she got 6,421 steps so far today. Her mother turns to her and then back, preferring to address her in the rearview mirror.

"What the fuck, Brianna?"

Her bank account sucks. No DMs, no texts.

"You ruined this. Your grandmother's nice night and all she's going through and you're getting high in my goddamn car."

"I'm not," she said.

"Disappearing all the time. No wonder you wanted to drive. Jesus, I thought there was just some idiot you wanted to talk to."

She fumbles for language, because her mother is commanding her to in this small, airless space. She wants her grandmother to tell her to stop. She wants the key in the ignition to turn. "Not high," she manages, because she has to say something.

"The disrespect you show me. Your grandmother. The un, the fucking *in*gratitude. You act like you're too fucking good for this family and then you do this. And boy did you pick a hell of a time to do it."

"That's enough, Mel," her grandmother says quietly. "Let's not end the night like this."

"But aren't you going to tell her?"

"No, Melanie. Not now, no. It was such a nice night."

"Oh, Mom," Brianna's mother says, and that's all she can manage before she begins to cry again. Nana puts a hand to her troubled daughter's back. "It's okay," she says. And then her mother knuckles her dripping nose, takes a few ragged breaths, and starts the car. It comes to Brianna, with a deep and sudden ache, why her grandmother is stepping down from her position as event coordinator of the Michigan Elvis Fan Club; why Leo Days said she could call on her Elvis family in the dark days; why her mom said she needed to get her ass home for ElvisFest.

The air-conditioning kicks in. The CD player picks up where it left off, mid-hymn.

Across the Midwest, mothers and grandmothers are pulling the bobby pins from their hair-spray-shellacked updos, rubbing slow circles of cold cream over their eyes. They're unzipping sparkly but sensible dresses in peony pink and dove gray, with short jackets that hide the flabby hang of their upper arms. Nails to match. Clutch bags for Kleenex and lipstick. Today, in the crying rooms of churches and in country-club ladies lounges they wept over their daughters, praised their beauty, fretted over their hair. They are so proud. They have paid for the weddings, paid for everything, the string quartet included. "Thank you for helping make this night special," they'll put in the notes of their Venmo payments once they've settled in their bathrobes on the couch or in the downy pile of their beds in houses like the houses of the girls Brianna went to school with, their big windows looking out on sweeping lawns or Lake St. Clair, open-plan kitchens with marble counters, stainless steel gleaming, upholstered chairs around the dining table. It occurs to Brianna now that, even playing Vivaldi, she is still one of the people who get a quick thank-you, like the women who come in once a week to scrub the toilet bowl and polish the furniture.

Detroit, viewed from the back seat of this silent car reeking of cannabis, feels endless. The artless hulk of the Renaissance Center and the warehouses and the junkyards with the cars stacked into the sky. The Fisher Plant with its windows broken and graffiti. Her grandmother dislodges something from her throat and spits it into a handkerchief. Brianna is crying now too. She's had so little and now she'll have even less.

Brianna's car is packed. She takes the bags from the trunk and puts them in her cello case, which now, too, smells like weed, and she worries over how she'll get the smell out by tomorrow, if her roommate has Febreeze or something, if that even works.

Brianna watches her speed. Every cop that appears in her rearview mirror makes her shift around on her tailbone. She grips the steering wheel at ten and two. She keeps her cell phone on silent in her purse, which is in the back seat. She ignores her dry mouth and her full bladder, willing herself across the state line and into Indiana. If she makes it back by two and falls asleep by three, she can get five hours of sleep.

So it isn't until she's nearly to Fort Wayne, so close, when she stops at a gas station. She drops to the toilet and her keys fall to the tile. She urinates with a force that aches. It feels like her bladder will never empty. Maybe there's something wrong with her. Maybe she'll never have children. And maybe that's fine, considering. She opens up her phone. There's an overdraft notification from her bank. Her grandmother says, *Text us when you get home Bri*. A group text notification from Dagyeom says, *Hey hope your grandma is okay but we decided to go with the new player for the rest of the summer,* and she studies the lines of the beaten floor tile, the impressions of so many dirty shoes, her Elvis keychain, until someone knocks on the door and tells her to hurry the fuck up. ⊙

Two short stories

James Yeh

PARABLE OF THE POND

Restless, a man—let's say it's a man—goes in search of a pond. He hasn't done any planning, but it's a short hike; anyway, he's got a map. He's following the trail, one red-marked tree trunk after another, so he calls his partner, five hours away, back in the city. It's been a minute, and soon he's absorbed in the news from home. Suddenly he realizes he's lost—no red marks, or blue, or white ones either. Somewhat abruptly, and with an irritation masking panic, he ends the call to reorient himself. But he still can't figure out which way to go. Eventually he comes upon a large, open field, with many tree stumps and fallen branches—this place calls to him. Pausing his search for the pond, the man settles on one of the stumps to record his thoughts on one of the notepads he's always carrying around. Meanwhile a tick has settled onto his pant leg; he's startled when he notices it and, with the back of his notebook, tries to crush it. But you can't crush a tick so easily. Doing so takes effort, and skill. Finally he's succeeded in flicking it off—goodbye, bug. Now he's ready to go back, pond be damned. But he can't find the way, so he chooses this time a blue marker. Out of the corner of his eye, he sees a glimmer—at last, after having given up all hope, there it is: the pond! A lesson in there somewhere, he thinks. He goes to the shimmering waters, elated, but when he gets there, the mosquitoes are too thick, and he can only stay for a moment. He takes a quick photo, then rushes back to where he came from.

SIGNS OF LIFE

That winter, the son goes back for two weeks to help his parents. His mother is ill, his father ill-tempered and, he feels, struggling with her care. At the hospital, people compliment him on his patience, or what appears to be patience, as he wheels his mother from one waiting room into the next.

These are the days of doctors' appointments and nights of crashing on a mattress on the floor in the small room above the garage, where the son's father has set him up.

One day the son is at his makeshift desk—the kind of folding table usually used for card games—when he spots a ladybug creeping along the windowpane. Wanting to save it, he improvises a carrier—two sheets of paper, a toilet-paper tube—and, with a tenderness that he believes is characteristic though is, actually, capricious—he brings the carrier outside, where the tiny creature inches off the page and onto the branch of a shrub as the son watches with triumph and wonder, the warm wash of all's well in the world.

Back at his folding-table desk, a less fuzzy feeling forms. On a hunch, the son goes over to the window. Sure enough, there on the sill, are dried husks, a veritable insect graveyard: silverfish, bees, even another ladybug, its body no longer red but now rust.

Is this the takeaway he seeks, dead bugs on a ledge?

And is this also why he persists in buying for his parents, despite his father's objection—"not enough space," he complains—so many potted plants and flowers, these arresting signs of life?

The son goes downstairs, listening for his mother's sounds. She's been laid up in bed, suffering from dizziness and a malignant growth in her abdomen—smaller than a ladybug at this stage, smaller than a flea—that won't be found until it's too late.

But, right now, the son's mother must still be asleep: the only sound around is from the TV, some finance program of his father's. The son hears from that distance the newscaster's falsely cheery voice: "the Fed response," "oil embargo," "buying opportunities," and his own response is to slink back, like a timid child or sulking teen, to his room above the garage.

Some weeks later, at a noisy bar in the city, where the son now lives, he tells the story of the ladybug and its multiple meanings. His friend, a young woman from a country people here are suspicious of, replies in poetic, accented English how you can only know what's what at the end, when all's been said and done.

The son agrees partway, though he's unsure why only partway. Is it because of hope, or helplessness? There is so much to feel helpless about, far less to be hopeful for.

But some things he holds out for still: the plight of a single bug, the extended life of a houseplant or a parent.

He wants to be someone who checks in on his parents without getting into a fight, a son who shows up, gently and attentively, and on this night, he is. ⊙

How it works

Ashleigh Bryant Phillips

It was the end of the night. We were all on our last leg. I was standing in a bar called the Turkey's Nest—in Williamsburg—talking to my friend Jimmy.

I was drinking water. Jimmy had a beer. We were looking at the TV. A commercial for the Marines came on. It was Veterans Day.

And I said, "I grew up with two boys who joined the Marines—Ryan and Ray Daughtry. They came into our class in the fifth grade. They were twins and dressed just alike…You know them shirts you can get in a pack at Walmart?—Like Hanes?"

"Yeah," said Jimmy.

"That's what Ryan and Ray wore every day, gray five-pack Hanes T-shirts. With Wrangler jeans and steel-toe boots. And they tucked their shirts into their jeans. Nobody else dressed like that… and they couldn't read that good. So remember when you'd be reading something in class and everybody would have to read out loud? Going down the rows, everybody reading a paragraph?"

"Yeah," Jimmy said.

"Well Ryan and Ray were a year older than all of us. They'd been held a year back already. And they couldn't read good and one day when it was Ray's turn to read, he didn't do it. The teacher said, *Ray, please start on page six* or whatever it was. And I won't never forget what he said. He looked up at her and said, *Make me*. None of us had ever heard that before."

"Damn," said Jimmy.

"I mean Ray wanted everybody to think he was tough. He was always doodling guns and stuff. Looking back on it now, it's fucked. I remember the boys told me that he was going around telling them that their daddy was in jail for murdering someone. But none of us believed it. We all just thought he was trying to look tough and all…But it wudent until I was grown and I was talking about Ryan and Ray to my mama and she said, *Oh yeah, their Daddy murdered a girl out in Roxobel.*"

"Damn," said Jimmy.

"He'd been having an affair with this girl and one night he killed her and came home with blood all over him. And he wouldn't tell his wife what had happened but she called the law anyways. And she left him that night, ran out with Ryan and Ray, they won't but two or something."

Jimmy didn't say anything, but I just kept going, "When they came to our class, their mama, Miss Cindy, had married a big farmer and he'd adopted the boys. She was really big into Christian radio. Everytime we had a field trip she'd drive because she had a Suburban and could haul us all and she'd always have the Christian radio playing."

Jimmy took the last swallow of his beer.

"And all that time, all the grown folks knew what happened. But they didn't tell any of us."

"And how's that make you feel now?" Jimmy asked me.

"I think I could have handled it."

"Yeah," Jimmy laughed.

I looked around and our friends were shooting pool or heading out to smoke cigarettes.

"Fuck man," I said. "All because of a Marines commercial."

"That's how it works," said Jimmy.

"That's how it works."

Jimmy gave me a hug and went out for a cigarette.

I put my hands in my new red coat. I'd just gotten it that day. It was designer. I'd never bought a designer coat before. The whole night everyone was telling me how they loved it.

After the Marines, Ryan and Ray came back home to farm peanuts. Their daddy died in prison.

And even if she wanted to, the girl he killed couldn't be there with me, galavanting New York City. She won't nothing now but the essential cog in the wheel to the story.

And there I was in the Turkey's Nest, looking for someone to take a picture of me—so I could remember the day I bought a red designer jacket. ⊙

A DAY IN THE LIFE AT HUB CITY PRESS
as told by ceiling rat
& JULIE JAREMA
CREEEaak
pat
pat
pat
DO YOU HEAR RUSTLING IN THE CEILING?
MAYBE WE HAVE A GHOST!
BUT MORE LIKELY A MOUSE OR A Rat...
YEAH, IT'S AN OLD BUILDING ANYTHING COULD BE UP THERE.
PACKING MATERI

MARKETING
① ARCS
② PACK
③ SEAL
④ LABEL
⑤ SHIP
PACKING MATERI/
(OUT OF MAILERS)
SLIIIDE
OH THANK YOU
WUT.
shhh
MAILERS
PRODUCTION
2025
ARCs
EVENTS/ WORKSHOPS
OPEN CALLS
BOOK DEADLINES
·crash course
·virtual book launch
·Curtis prize
ACQUISITIONS
2026 novel?
poetry contracts
·sales conference prep
·spring '26 metadata
'25 to printer
·print fall 25

BOOKSHOP SHIFT & SOCIAL MEDIA

EDITORIAL & LUNCH BREAK

PUBLICITY

YOU'RE SUCH A SMALL TEAM. HOW DO YOU DO IT ALL?
IT'S A MYSTERY, EVEN TO US.

Fleas

Kate Arden McMullen

The dog had fleas. There was nothing we could do about this. It had already happened. We kept it off the furniture and we sprayed the house with stuff from a bottle everyday. We were diligent. We scratched the little red bites on each other's arms and legs and waited for the fleas to die.

The vet gave us pills to feed the dog. We folded slices of cheese around them to fool the dog. Sometimes this worked. Sometimes we sat on the floor beside the dog and opened its mouth to drop the pills in. We had to get our hand just right around the muzzle to open the mouth and get the pills between the teeth. The dog never seemed to mind this, but we kept on with the cheese. It seemed more dignified.

The fleas left the dog but not the house. There was no pill to kill the couch and carpet fleas. We searched the internet to confirm this. We spent as much time out of the house with the dog as possible. This turned out to be good for us. We found a new dog park by the river. We found a pet-friendly coffee shop were we could read and write and talk together. People came up to pet the dog. We said its name and breed. We let children touch its wet nose.

We let the fleas live in the house. We hoped they hadn't laid eggs and that those eggs hadn't hatched. Then we stopped thinking about it. We visited both our parents. We took camping trips. The dog put its head out the window, and we stopped bothering with the cheese. We gave it all the pills, and it stopped scratching, and we stopped too. Our bites healed, our skin smoothed. The flea eggs settled into our hardwood floors.

In the summer we returned. We had forgotten about the fleas in all we learned about each other, and the people we had met. On the second day in the house the flea eggs hatched, and we woke itching in the night, and yelled at each other while we sprinkled pink chemicals we bought at the pet store, and the smell trapped itself in the corners of the house and gave us gnawing headaches and made the dog's eyes water, and we grew tired and pale and lonely.

The pink chemicals worked. The smell eventually dissipated. We bought a new cordless vacuum cleaner, the one we saw on television. We held hands at parties and the dog slept between us at night.

We went on camping trips in the fall and wished the whole time we were home. When we were home, we wished we were somewhere else. The dog needed teeth pulled but neither of us had the money.

We lived in the house and the fleas came with the seasons. They took part in our arguments and our lovemaking, in our together and aloneness, in our hair and skin. We could never stop thinking of each other, of the bites on our knees. ⊙

Hungry

Halle Hill

To stay out of the pantry on a Friday night, I went downstairs to smoke out of the big corner window. It was the last week of May, the last week of my miserable eighth-grade year, and come fall, I'd be in high school. Daddy was still in the hospital recovering from surgery and would be released in a week or so—a few days before my graduation. I was fiddling for my cigarettes, about to reach the bottom step, when I heard panting like dogs in heat. Ms. Glenda straddled both sides of my mother's hips, her hair was wet with sweat. My mother was crying. Ms. Glenda cupped her hand under my mother's chin and kissed her eyes. I turned around and snuck back upstairs while one of them moaned like she wasn't hiding in our basement. Daddy didn't need any more shock. I sucked my stomach in then pushed it all down deep.

"Bad blood," as Aunt Esther called it, ran on both sides of our family. It crept up on Daddy last year, and despite the warnings, all it took was a pin-prick wound for him to come undone. In March, he developed gout, then in April nerve damage—

neuropathy—in that same foot; it started to tingle and then he lost most of the feeling altogether. Then in early May the back of his heel got cut, nothing more than a scrape. He didn't feel it, and soon after it got infected and turned into an open sore that turned gangrene, which traveled up the appendage, which led to his foot getting cut off at the ankle.

This all led to me going to my first meeting before eighth grade even let out for summer. As soon as I saw Daddy come into our house with bandages where his foot used to be, I knew someone had to change.

Aunt Esther wanted me to keep my vitality early in life. "You're too young for all this weight. I know we run big, but you have to get slim," she told me a million times. She prodded me to the meetings for months. I hadn't wanted to go. I couldn't imagine going to another place where people judged my body. But I'd finally caved. I thought of Aunt Esther as more of a mother than my own. She looked more like me and Daddy anyway.

I looked out the window while Aunt Esther listened to Destiny's Child on low. We drove twenty minutes down a country road to Second United Methodist, a cold, castle-type church with white Jesus in stained glass. Aunt Esther tapped her thumbs on the steering wheel and cleaned some waffle from in between her teeth. She took me to breakfast at Denny's earlier in the morning for one last hoorah. We wore matching airbrush T-shirts from our spring-break trip to Ruby Falls. I felt excited about the new me; I imagined the fat melting off my waist like butter.

"Are you nervous?" Aunt Esther asked in the car. Her stomach bubbled around the seat belt.

"No, not really."

"It's okay if you are. This is a safe space. No one will judge you." She looked over at me and patted my shoulder. I didn't believe her but it felt good to be in her car, just us, moving away from home.

"Eh, I feel fine." I looked out the window and saw a picket sign: WEIGHT WATCHERS SLIM DOWN! TURN HERE.

"Well, here we go. If at any time you feel uncomfortable, let me know. Squeeze my hand three times, and we'll leave. You hear me?"

I nodded and slowly made my way out the door and into the basement's rec room.

I knew I had to get smaller for two reasons.

The first reason: For him. Last summer the doctor gave him the diagnosis. They'd been warning him about it for years. His daddy had it, his daddy's daddy had had it, and so on. The doctor told our family Daddy would have to change his lifestyle tremendously or things could turn quick: lost eyesight, kidney problems, cirrhosis, lost limbs, heart attack, even stroke. As the doctor drilled him, I looked over at my father and saw strong parts of me reflected back: his smooth, pecan face, long legs, broad shoulders, and dark eyelashes. I looked back at my mother: so fit, her eyes severe, disappointed. I wondered what would become of us.

When Mom brought Daddy home from his surgery, he tried to have some humor about it. He made jokes about himself having been All-American, a Wharton bigwig, the strongest star-length softball coach, and whatnot. "Now look at me," he said.

Neighbors visited and brought us food after the procedure. They made low-carb stews and veggie stir-fries. Glenda came over, too, and offered to be helpful: "Just tell me what to do, whatever you need." She brought a sugar-free angel food cake, hugged all of us with a bony warmth, and wiped down our counters. She said she would be there as much as she could to help out. She and my mother barely made eye contact, and I wondered if I really saw what I remembered.

The second reason: I had something to prove. My mother eternally harped on me about my weight, nagging me, squishing my sides, only letting me have my sweets on special occasions. Her body weighed her down so she couldn't imagine mine as anything other than a burden. I'd never seen her face bare. She touched up her makeup before going to bed and believed in preventative Juvederm at the ripe age of thirty-five. Any time I whined about feeling insecure, she put a hand to my face and scoffed, "You think you have it bad, you just don't know." As a child, on Saturdays, her mother woke her and her sisters up and brought them to the laundry room in their white sleep slips. She placed them on top of their yellow top-load Maytag, then started an empty wash cycle. As the machine moved, she circled where they jiggled—"improvement areas," she called them.

Mom had been hospitalized twice for anorexia in high school. Ran so long and so hard she'd permanently lost the cartilage in her knees—at forty she had already had the left one replaced. Outside of her food issues, she felt effervescent—smart, funny, larger than life—but between the two of us, because I wasn't the size she needed me to be, she felt bitter, mean about food, and mad about me. "Ten more pounds and she'll roll," I heard her say to her sister on the phone. She'd even taped WordArt reminders on my bathroom mirror and above the left door handle on the fridge: NOTHING TASTES AS GOOD AS THIN FEELS.

And she wasn't the only one. It seemed like everybody had something to say about my big bones: my teachers, my friends' mothers, the mailman. Earlier this year, at Katie Castellano's sleepover, after we played light as a feather, stiff as a board, we played a new game called "guess how much," where each of the girls got on the scale in Katie's mother's bathroom while the others wrote on slips of paper how much they thought the girl on the scale weighed. We folded the slips of paper and placed them in a fishbowl, then watched with wide eyes while she stepped on and the numbers calibrated. Even the girl getting weighed herself would step on the scale backward, and someone would hold the fishbowl out to her and she would drop her guess in the bowl, too. After we saw the number, Katie would scoop out the guesses and stand in front of us and read us our weight. Whoever guessed closest won. Of course, the real winner weighed the least. My self-estimate? Fifteen pounds too generous, and I lost the game by about forty pounds. I stood there with them watching me in silence, mortified.

Walking into the meeting, I barely noticed anyone around me. Instead, my whole body focused on shrinking.

ARE YOU HUNGRY FOR LIFE? Neon-pink, Comic Sans flyers interrogated me across the walls.

Aunt Esther walked me to the check-in counter to get measured, and I tucked in line behind her.

The acrylics on the check-in lady's hand were perfect, so pink. The French tips were sharply squared and bright, bleach white. The gloss on them looked wealthy. The way they sat on her hands looked so familiar, and I realized they were the same ones I saw running down my mother's brown back in the basement.

"Welcome to the first day of your new life!" Glenda said to me and Aunt Esther while shaking our hands. I felt clammy against her lotioned palm.

Hospitality reeked out of Glenda, those bright teeth stark against her shiny skin. Tide detergent wafted off her body and into my face while I looked at her, my eyes narrow with knowing, and she glanced back at me, just a nobody. Ms. Glenda signed me in and made me a name tag, then gave me my introductory packet.

WELCOME TO THE NEW YOU! it said on the glossy outside, with a photo of a slim Asian woman smiling while eating a forkful of salad. I opened it and filled out the questionnaire.

On a scale of 1 to 10, how much does food control your life? 10
On a scale of 1 to 10, how motivated do you feel to exercise? 3
On a scale of 1 to 10, how would you rate your self-esteem, right now? 2
On a scale of 1 to 10, how attached do you feel to sugar? 10
One a scale of 1 to 10, how much are you ready to change (p.s. The only acceptable answer is 10!)? 10

After I filled it out, Ms. Glenda took my pamphlet and told me when it was my turn to step on the scale.

"What about my clothes?"

I wondered if anything I was wearing had been in the pile on the laundry-room floor that night.

"Yes, ma'am! You're a smart one. We take off four pounds in place of being fully clothed. That's the one great thing about these meetings—you can always count on losing four pounds!" She winked and gestured for me to step on. Her smell slapped me in the face again.

I looked down expecting to see a number, but the screen was taped over with pink construction paper that read YOU ARE BEAUTIFUL! with heart stickers plastered around. Ms. Glenda looked at my weight on the computer screen and tapped it with her shiny index nail. She bit her lip a little, then smiled, scribbled some numbers in my pamphlet, and ushered me into the big meeting room with a skylight the size of heaven.

Aunt Esther and I sat together in the third row from the back after we grabbed our refreshments. There were maybe twenty other women, mostly Aunt Esther's age. A few pudgy twentysomethings lurked in the back rows. I kept wondering if I was crazy; if I was sure I saw Ms. Glenda a few nights before, in between my mother's legs. I went to get something to drink.

I saw lemonade. The meeting was off to a great start. It was Crystal Light, raspberry flavored, and Ms. Glenda and the other leaders cut up individual Atkins bars into mini baking cups: the option of "mocha mint" or "peanut butter chocolate chip" for us all to choose.

The meeting started with the Slideshow of Success. Ms. Glenda came up to the front, but this time she was what my father would call "deadly serious." With the clicker in her hand, she turned the projector on, and it opened to a photo of her pushing 300 pounds. Then she pressed the clicker and showed another one of her after she lost 150 of them. She preached to us about the importance of self-responsibility.

"It's all about willpower."

"*Only YOU can make the change.*"

The room erupted in clapping for Ms. Glenda while she mouthed, "Thank you, thank you," over and over again, with her hand on her chest. From my seat I counted four of her ribs. All of us newbies were hooked, as she talked about how Weight Watchers gave her ownership over all the areas of her life she couldn't control; it gave her a sense of strength. I was burning in my seat, ready for my miracle.

After the presentation, there was a part of the meeting where anyone could walk up to the microphone in the middle of the room and testify about their program successes. One woman, Daisy, stood up and said she lost her first five pounds. She lifted her shirt and tugged at the waistband of her khakis to show us the slack. Everyone gasped, which made her smile and caused her to lean into the mic closer.

"How were you able to do it, girl?" Aunt Esther asked from the audience. I hated how friendly she could be.

"Sticking to my low-point foods, and substituting sugar-free everything! It's all about low-carb for me!"

Ms. Glenda came up beside her and congratulated Daisy by rubbing her shoulders and whispering in her ear. Daisy beamed.

I took mental notes on everything I learned that day: drinking hot water could make you feel fuller longer; Parkay Butter Spray was program friendly; sugar-free Jello with unsweetened whipped cream could fill the fructose hole; and, perhaps most important, being fat was the worst thing any woman could ever be.

At my graduation ceremony, Mom and Daddy and Aunt Esther sat close to the stage and waved to me when it was my turn to walk across. Mom was there taking pictures of me, the flash bright from the wind-up camera she bought just an hour before at the corner store. Daddy sat in his chair and clapped for me the loudest, wearing a bow tie the same shade of purple as my middle school. I felt embarrassed in my women's size-eight dress. All my friends were still in pre-teen sizes. I already wore a B-cup bra.

Daddy had been ordered by the doctor to stay in his wheelchair, and me and Mom tried a million different ways to hide his loss. We couldn't afford any type of decent prosthetic in our wildest dreams, so we did the next best thing and got crafty. We tried filling his slacks with tufts of stuffing and attached his dress shoe at the bottom, but it wouldn't hold. Eventually, we made the painful decision to cut his pant leg and bind it right below where the ankle would have been, securing it with a black rubber band.

As I walked across, he smiled from ear to ear, but when I looked over at him again his face had dropped, his shoulders were drooped, and he was wiping tears away. I couldn't tell if they were the kind that came from great pride or unbearable grief.

When summer break finally started, Aunt Esther and I went to Weight Watchers every week. I had a goal to lose thirty-five pounds before high school that fall, and she dreamt of losing fifteen. I begged Mom to help me buy better foods and fill the fridge with them, which pleased her. I ate steamed broccoli and cod with lemon pepper, stopped having added sugar, and only drank water if I couldn't get a diet soda.

The weight fell off pretty quickly. Daddy got worse.

With his illness rocketing since the amputation, they placed him on injectable insulin. The vials sat in the fridge next to my Gatorade Zero, and every morning, I watched him drink his coffee, then pinch a fold on the side of his stomach while he jabbed the clear liquid into himself.

Daddy's days seemed perpetually dreary. He became obsessed with the statistics against him. Wheeling around the kitchen, he would say them out loud over and over again: *Black men have a 50 percent chance in developing diabetes over any other group of people. People with diabetes are two times more likely to get depression. People who get an amputation from a diabetes complication have a 75 percent rate of losing another body part.*

He couldn't shake it. He and my mother would fight about it. She called him pessimistic. He said he was accepting of the inevitable.

I didn't understand how it changed so quickly, how he could have let himself get this bad. It started last year, when he got laid off from his C-suite job. He came home different. Before this he seemed perfect; my safe, reliable, Disney-movie father. A good dad, he ran two miles a day, wore the same dry-cleaned clothes, told dumb jokes, took the cars to get the oil changed. We would take walks sometimes in the evenings, get ice cream, and watch Turner Classic Movies. But one day he gave up. And no matter how much I asked about what happened, no one would tell me why.

After he got the diagnosis last summer, Daddy and Mom started sleeping in separate rooms. Mom started slamming doors. And he started staying at home more. He quit asking if I wanted to run to the store with him and stopped prodding at me to get off the computer. He came home late, and drank Black and Tans on the couch. Some days, I'd tried to get him to go with me down by the dock and watch the water to cheer him up, but all he wanted was his time. He got so thirsty all of a sudden and went through pints of iced tea, complained of exhaustion, and kept rushing to the restroom.

Daddy became erratic. His moods made him throw his pill bottles against the wall in the kitchen, weep uncontrollably, or become withdrawn. Most days he would sit on the couch with his crutches laid to the side and watch Lifetime movies with a flat look in his eye.

Ms. Glenda was winning. Ms. Glenda was ruining my family. Ms. Glenda from down the street, married with two kids, was lying to my father's face. Ms. Glenda, head of the cross-country team parent association with Revlon blonde hair, was sleeping with my mother and didn't feel bad about it.

I dragged myself across the world that summer. I was too young for a gym membership, so I started walking everywhere. At Weight Watchers, Ms. Glenda mentioned getting a pedometer and walking 10,000 steps a day, so I upped mine to 19,000. I walked laps in the backyard with my Discman and sports bra. Back and forth, I turned golden in the summer sun. I watched myself in the reflection off our sliding glass door and hoped I could whittle away.

I made a friend in the meetings, Rachel Goldstein, who was a rising sophomore and lived in Sequoia Hills. She had lost forty-seven pounds the summer before. Every morning, she started coming over and pacing with me, both of us wearing matching

Puma sweatbands while we talked about periods and third base and how to check our BMIs. She also taught me about sugar-free gum and how to vomit with the back of a toothbrush. Under the dogwood trees, while we sweated, she told me stories about her new twenty-three-year-old boyfriend, Johnny, and the vibrator he bought her from Spencer's.

While we paced and paced, Daddy wasted. Despite his reluctance, me and Mom lugged him to the doctor as often as we could, and we learned the new medication had a potential side effect of major depressive disorder.

Most evenings he sat around, dumbstruck, in an SWV T-shirt he wore for a few days straight, collar stretched out. Mom was nowhere to be found in the evenings, running her endless list of errands. She was nicer to me, would see me around, put her hands on my waist, squeezing, and say, "Finally, there's my pretty girl," in passing as we went our separate ways. I lost track of the days altogether.

I slept over at Rachel's house as much as possible. I was sick of seeing my dad so pitiful, and I was obsessed with disappearing. Her house was exactly three miles away, so I walked to it as much as I could. It was nice to have a best friend. Rachel's parents divorced a few years earlier, so just her father and she lived there. Mr. Goldstein worked bicoastally for a Fortune 500 consulting firm, which left Rachel mostly alone, save for her 7,000-square-foot home and her nanny Delores, who drank Rolling Rock beers and watched *Days of Our Lives* while she rested her eyes.

Before Aunt Esther picked us up for the meetings, Rachel and I went to her bathroom and made ourselves throw up anything in our stomachs. After, we took a tape measure to our waists. Hers stayed at nineteen inches, mine not budging at twenty-one. On bad days she'd hold my hand or put an arm around me. "We'll do better tomorrow." My throat burned with bile like I'd swallowed the sun.

On good days, while Aunt Esther blew on the horn, we would look at ourselves in the mirror and sling our arms around each other, taking turns, standing hip bone to hip bone, calling one another "simply divine."

Mom and Aunt Esther started talking a lot in other rooms when I was home. They would whisper so quietly, making hushed noises in the guest room, then come out, wiping their eyes quickly.

Other than doctor appointments, Dad hadn't left the house in seven weeks.

My breath smelled perpetually sour, and I wore heavy black clothes all day in the sun to make me sweat as much as possible. One day when I walked over to Rachel's estate, Delores opened the door and wouldn't pull it past the chain lock. "Rachel's not having company right now. She's out of town." She glared at me. I asked when she would get back, and Delores told me not for a long while. It turned out Rachel's dad was more in tune than we expected, and she had been filling him in on our concerning behavior. Delores handed me a glossy brochure for the Young Roses Treatment Facility for Anorexia Nervosa and Bulimia, told me to please take care of myself, then shut the door. They had sent Rachel away to the West Coast campus in Malibu. I stood there for a while and stared at placid pictures of a rocky beach and the big, blue Pacific.

That night, Mr. Goldstein called our landline and said Rachel wouldn't be talking to me for a while. He asked me to put one of my parents on the phone, but I told him my parents were never home.

School started soon, and I beat my goal: I lost around forty pounds from May to September and mastered any type of pangs with my mints and cigarettes on the hour.

Fluid ballooned around Daddy's ankle and his wrists. I could hear him breathing, or trying to breathe, his mouth wide and gasping as he complained all day of his tongue feeling like chalk. He wouldn't even move from the couch, sometimes for almost two days. When I would ask him, "Daddy, don't you need to use the restroom?" he would chuckle and say, "Actually, dear, I don't. Even if I wanted to piss, nothing would come out."

The last time we ate dinner as a family, Mom and Daddy asked me if I was happy about going to high school with my new buddy soon. I shrugged.

He quit eating. I cried myself to sleep.

Aunt Esther was the one to finally tell me it was kidney failure. She was taking me to my final Weight Watchers meeting of the summer, a week before school started, and I was smacking sugar-free Dentyne Ice, imagining it as a whole cheese pizza. When Aunt Esther missed the turn to the Methodist church, I figured she wasn't paying attention. She kept driving up the parkway. I figured we were going someplace else. We pulled over at a stop to watch the mountains, and we got out and sat on a bench, the same one we would come to from time to time when I was a child.

"Now dear, I need to tell you something," she said.

"Okay."

"Your father, he isn't doing too well."

"Mhmm."

"Okay. So, listen good and hard to me. He is in acute kidney failure and only has a few months left to live, if he can't get a transplant."

"Mhmm." I reached for my pedometer. Only 9,000 steps so far, *shit*. It should have been around 15k. I'd been up since five that morning running the numbers: pacing, doing crunches, hopping on and off and on and off the scale.

"The transplant list has so many people on it, it is not likely that he will get one in time. Do you understand what I'm saying to you?"

My ears started to ring, and I felt full from my chest to my toes. I shoved four pieces of gum in the back of my mouth, and a piece of foil caught in between the pieces.

"I'm so sorry, sweetie. We didn't know how to tell you. I wish I would have told you sooner, but your mom and I were in total shock."

A few days later, I went to drop a postcard off for Rachel at the mailbox, and I was trying to enjoy the breeze in my hair, trying to think of him with me. Daddy liked summer. He used to take me for sunset walks in the summer.

When I got back in the house, I thought Daddy was just asleep, so I didn't bother him. I walked over to him and pulled the blanket up to his shoulders and cut the TV off. He looked okay, peaceful really, and I felt punched in the gut when I looked at him lying there on our old leather sectional. I thought of our summers on the Outer Banks, looking for creatures in the low tide at night, buckets in our hands and stars above us. How could this be the same man who held me above the waves until I loved the water as much as he did? I thought about calling out my mother's name to see if she was around. I checked the fridge to test myself and saw a note she left. OUT WITH GIRLFRIENDS FOR DINNER. TXT IF YOU NEED ME!

I needed to make sure that Daddy took his meds, so I went to wake him up and that's when I realized how hard it was for him to breathe. He wheezed like a fish, his lips turned blue.

I was the only one who rode with him in the ambulance.

Aunt Esther made it there right as they put the intubation tubes in. They were able to get him stable, but soon after they placed him in a coma so his body could regulate. For a man who seemed unbreakable, he looked impossibly weak as he laid hooked up to machines that breathed for him. The doctor said he might be able to improve temporarily, but not for long.

With his need for the transplant and this damage to his immune system, our days together were numbered. I kept waiting for Daddy to open his eyes.

Everything was about willpower. My wants were just an illusion to be managed.

Any cravings signaled a deeper need.

When I wanted sugar, I really needed fruit.

When I was craving salt, I really just felt thirsty.

The trick was to master my desire, that's what I learned in the meetings. I needed to trick my mind. You gotta know when you're really hungry and when you just think you are.

It was nearly an hour after we arrived when Ms. Glenda and my mother showed up to the hospital. My eyes burned out of my skull in rage. Mom was beside herself, demanding to know the details, fat tears down her face: Where was he when I found him? Did he take his insulin? Did I check on him? *Selfish,* she called me. She acted a fool in the hospital room, sobbing, then yelling, then sobbing again, while my father laid stiff on those starchy hospital sheets.

Ms. Glenda came over to my mother and held her tenderly, leaned her whole body against her and whispered something in my mother's ear. She held onto the back of her neck, and moved the hair out of her face.

"You've gotta be fucking kidding me," Aunt Esther sighed, standing. She paced the room.

But my mother didn't even look at her, and kept holding on to Ms. Glenda for support. Ms. Glenda heard it, though.

"Esther, I can't imagine what you're going through. I promise I'm here." She looked over at him with puppy eyes.

My aunt started saying something about her nerve, but a

nurse walked in and she stopped.

I walked over to Daddy and tried to feel the warmth in his hands. I squeezed three times, hoping he'd squeeze back and let me know this was one of his jokes, that he was ready to go home. My mother continued to wail into Ms. Glenda's arms, and I kept squeezing, trying to move the life back into him.

The nurse checked his oxygen line. She looked at us. I froze like I was running in quicksand. She checked his pulse, and made some notes, then left without saying anything. The doctor came in and said he had to share some news.

Aunt Ester pulled me away.

"We should get some fresh air, baby," she cooed. "That sounds nice, right? Come on with me, let's take a break."

I checked my pedometer: only 11,000. I needed to take a few more. Together, we walked out past my mother and Ms. Glenda, down the stairs, out the exit doors and into the dark night.

I kept thinking about what Glenda taught us in that first seminar (was that really a few months ago?): how to keep it off, the BIG secret. Aunt Ester had tried that day to grab my hand in the pew, but I'd moved it away from her while I zeroed in and held my breath. Glenda kept telling us it was all in the mind.

Nothing tastes as good as thin feels.

Did Glenda tell this to my mother? Or did my mother tell it to her?

You must change. You can disappear.

You have to find the will to fill the void, then make it so. ⊙

Religious group formed around hurricanes protest infrastructure improvements

Reyes Ramirez

Gyralism, a growing belief within the Gulf Coast, opposes changes to road infrastructure and drainage on the basis of religious grounds.

September 38, 2060
Updated 7:07 PM

During the March 34th meeting of Houston City Council's public comments section, a member of the Church of Gyralism spoke against an ordinance to inject an unprecedented $10 billion to renovate drainage systems and road infrastructure throughout the City. The spokesperson represented over 150 members crowding the council chambers and the exterior of City Hall.

The ordinance comes as a result of consecutive years of rising flood waters reaching up to nearly 120 inches of rain that have caused over a trillion dollars of damage to homes, businesses, and infrastructure that has collectively displaced nearly 3 million people and killed over 2,000. Funds will be used to enhance sewage systems, plant supertrees and turn abandoned lots into drainage facilities. Changes will take approximately 20 years to implement and require swathes of roads to be shut down and for neighborhoods to be temporarily relocated.

"This ordinance is a spit in the face of Gyre," said Sondra Aguasclaras, an apostle of the church, during her three-minute statement. "To believe that this will be enough to stop what's coming is not only a waste of our taxpayer dollars but an open insult to the power of Gyre without addressing the fundamental basis of her power."

"Though I understand and identify with your concerns," At-Large Council Member #22 Raul Ramirez said, "What you're saying is nonsense. I've spoken with our true Lord, and he says it's people like you that hold our progress back. Ya'll should be ashamed."

"Though I understand and identify with your concerns, too," District L Council Member Teisha Brown added, "it's important to consider the balance of our financial reality and our needs, of which there are plenty. This is the best path forward for Houston. Please contribute to this conversation constructively. Not like this. Whatever this is."

After Aguasclaras was dismissed from the podium, she and the other church members marched from the building to sit cross-legged in seemingly random clusters in the City Hall plaza around the reflection pond; after a moment, the members began rocking back and forth and spoke in incongruent chants to themselves, some screaming or whispering into the pond's shivering surface.

The Church of Gyralism has roots back to 2005 in the wake of Hurricane Katrina, when founder Rita Robinson evacuated to Houston after her home was devastated in New Orleans. Robinson built a life in Houston thereafter, getting married, having a daughter, and starting a brick-and-mortar fusion Tex-Mex/Cajun restaurant in the DowRiv neighborhood, in what was once known as the East End. That is, until Hurricane Harvey in 2017 destroyed her new home in Health District II, what was once known as Kashmere Gardens, causing her to close down her restaurant.

"My mother was a resilient woman," Aguasclaras said. "She began this Church after we lost our home and restaurant. It was in this state of grieving from immense loss that she found renewal and hope. That if she'd lost everything again and again, she could be reborn again and again. She wants everyone to find peace in loss, as she had to. Though she has since returned to the sea, the power of her grief and hope lives on."

The Church of Gyralism currently has a space, demarcated by their famous two mirrored cones converging upon a circle symbol, in what was once a community college center, a medical clinic and a brewery complex along I-45S now flanked by a liquor store, several chain restaurants and a research center to study displacement. The members delight in this arrangement.

"Gyralism teaches us to consider the intersections of destiny and our positionality within space and time," Grace Montoya said, a senior member of the Church. "In a weather event people and things are smashed and clumped together in contexts they wouldn't otherwise be, like cars inside living rooms, trees in power plants, people, living and dead, packed into empty malls. I had to sleep in a tax office for days after Tropical Storm Steve II. What was thought to be unimaginable is now normal. We're no longer in denial that this is the future."

There are still temporary sites of development that have remained dilapidated for the last several years, some reaching as far back as 15 years since Derecho Dave III devastated sections of South Houston. The Church of Gyralism incorporates this fact of Gulf Coast life into their practices.

For example, the Church of Gyralism's space is filled with furnishings salvaged and restored from members' devastated homes: couches patched together with jeans and nets; hanging lamps composed of rope with beer and water bottles; tables repaired with mismatched woods; and carpets of disharmonious colors littering the floors. One room contained piles of electronics they had repaired using spare parts from disposal sites.

"We never know who will be displaced next," said Taya Montemayor, a new convert. "I joined after moving here for work since Snow Vortex Mario in Beaumont. They gave me everything I needed to start a home, things that my elders had told me were normal to have back then: a fridge, a microwave, a TV."

Upon closer inspection, no church members, even church leaders, are dressed alike. They reuse salvaged clothes so that no members feel less welcome than others. In fact, church leader Aguasclaras was dressed in torn jeans, a shirt from a career fair 15 years ago, a green-and-pink flannel shirt and purple plastic shoes as she addressed the City Council.

"When you lose everything, anything is a blessing, mi mama would say," Aguasclaras said.

Another room contained a library of photo albums, yearbooks, and funeral programs found in disposal sites and dumps in case they could one day be found by those who had lost them. Record keeping and memories are important to church members, having a daily practice wherein a member enters a sensory deprivation tank while other members form a circle around them. The member in the tank begins telling a story while others listen seated with their legs crossed and eyes closed. This is so other members will keep any knowledge or memory from others should they ever be lost to a disaster.

A core belief that Gyralism is rumored to maintain is that hurricanes are celestial events, that the eyes of storms are portals to different realities. The gyres referenced in Gyralist symbols show how hurricanes converge alternate dimensions.

"The funnel of a gyre is a nexus point, our reality to be exact, that a hurricane disrupts so as to let us acces . . . ," an alleged document states, albeit received incomplete.

Aguasclaras would not confirm or deny these claims. Aguasclaras also clarified that the facility isn't a worship space and that more sacred practices are reserved to church members' homes to "build community and facilitate vulnerability."

Though Aguasclaras won't reveal specific membership numbers, the Church of Gyralism would confirm a record of new converts, as much as 10,000 new members across their branches in Houston, Galveston, Savannah, New Orleans, Miami, and more within the wake of Hurricane Noah III in August 2059 that left over 5 million people displaced in the Gulf Coast region.

The Church of Gyralism thoroughly rejects the label of doomsday cult, which it has been labeled as by government officials.

"How can we be a doomsday cult if we are just living our lives in the face of what we know is happening and what will come?" Aguasclaras said. "The true members of a doomsday cult are those who want to continue to uphold that all this is not really happening."

Experts agree that another disaster is imminent.

"We forsee more devastating weather events this year that we need to take very seriously," Professor of Atmospheric Sciences Roberta Sweeney at Houston University said. "It's no longer a matter of if, but when a global catastrophe will occur. Only by making major changes to institutional practices can we maybe save what's left."

While both critics and supporters agree that this ordinance is not enough to address larger issues of flooding and the rising number of weather disasters, it is the only government effort thus far to directly address infrastructure concerns. Last year, Houston experienced a record 12 weather events.

"This is better than nothing, I'm telling you," Houston Mayor Jeff Jeffries said. "The alternative to this is that we don't do a damn thing, and the majority of voters voted for me to do something. This is that something."

Jeffries was absent from the City Council meeting to accompany police on a sweep operation of an unhoused encampment near the NH 615 expansion site that has remained stalled for the last four years. The encampment numbers reached nearly 1,000 residents.

The ordinance is set to be voted upon next week. By law, no more public comments are allowed. ⊙

Show-and-tell

George Singleton

I wasn't old enough to know that my father couldn't have obtained a long-lost letter from famed lovers Heloise and Peter Abelard, and since European history wasn't part of my third-grade curriculum, I really felt no remorse in bringing the handwritten document—on lined and hole-punched Blue Horse filler paper—announcing its value, and reading it to the class on Friday show-and-tell. My classmates—who would all later grow up to be idiots, in my opinion, since they feared anything outside of South Carolina in general and my hometown of Forty-Five in particular, thus making them settle down exactly where they got trained, thus shrinking the gene pool even more—brought the usual: starfishes and conch shells bought in Myrtle Beach gift shops, though claimed to have been found personally during summer vacation; Indian-head pennies given as birthday gifts by grandfathers; the occasional pet gerbil, corn snake, or tropical fish. My father instructed me how to read the letter, what words to stress, when to pause. I, of course, protested directly after the dry run. Some of the words and phrases reached beyond my vocabulary. The general tone of the letter, I knew, would only get me playground-taunted by boys and girls alike. My father told me to pipe down and read louder. He told me to use my hands better and got out a metronome.

I didn't know that my father—a "widower" is what he instructed me to call him, although everyone knew how Mom ran off to Nashville and hadn't died—had once dated Ms. Suber, my teacher. My parents' pasts never came up in conversation, even after my mother ended up tending bar at a place called the Merchant's Lunch on Lower Broad more often than she sang on various honky-tonk stages, waiting for representation by a man who would call her the next Patsy Cline. No, the prom night and homecoming of my father's senior year in high school with Ms. Suber never leaked out in our talks, whether we ate supper in front of the television screaming at Walter Cronkite or played pinball down at the Sunken Gardens Lounge.

I got up in front of the class. I knew that a personal, caring, loving, benevolent God didn't exist, seeing as I had prayed that my classmates would spill over their allotted time, et cetera, et cetera, and then we'd go to recess, lunch, and then sit through one of the mandatory filmstrips each South Carolina elementary school student underwent weekly on topics as tragic and diverse as Friendship, Fire Safety, Personal Hygiene, and Bee Stings. "I have a famous letter written from one famous person to another famous person," I said.

Ms. Suber held her mouth in a tiny O. Nowadays I realize that she held beauty, but at the time she was just another very old woman in front of an elementary school class, her corkboard filled with exclamation marks. She wasn't but thirty-five, really. Ms. Suber motioned for me to edge closer to the music stand she normally used on Recorder Day. "And what are these famous people's names, Mendal?"

Ricky Hutton, who'd already shown off a ship in a bottle that he didn't make but said he did, yelled out, "My father has a letter from President Johnson's wife thanking him for picking up litter."

"My grandma sent me a birthday card with a two-dollar bill inside," said Libby Belcher, the dumbest girl in the class, who later went on to get a doctorate in education and then become superintendent of the school district.

I stood there with my folded document. Ms. Suber said, "Go on."

"I forget who wrote this letter. I mean, they were French people."

"Might it be Napoleon and Josephine?" Ms. Suber wore a smirk that I would see often in my life, from women who immediately recognized any untruth I chose to tell.

I said, "My father told me, but I forget. It's not signed or anything," which was true.

Ms. Suber pointed at Billy Gilliland and told him to quit throwing his baseball in the air, a baseball supposedly signed by Shoeless Joe Jackson that none of us believed in, seeing as the signature was printed, at best. We never relented on Gilliland, and later on he plain used the ball in pickup games until the cover wore off.

I unfolded the letter and read, "'My dearest?'"

"These were French people writing in English, I suppose," Ms. Suber said.

I nodded. I said, "They were smart, I believe. 'I want to tell you that if I live to be a hundred I won't meet another man like you. If I live to be a hundred there shall be no love to match ours.'"

The entire class began laughing, of course. My face reddened. I looked at Ms. Suber, but she concentrated on her shoe. "That guy who wrote that 'How Do I Love Thee' poem has nothing on us, my sugar-booger baby."

"That's enough," Ms. Suber belted out. "You can sit down, Mendal."

I pointed at the letter. I had another dozen paragraphs to go, some of which rhymed. I hadn't gotten to the word "throbbing," which showed up fourteen times. "I'm not making any of this up," I said. I walked two steps toward my third-grade teacher, but she stood up and told everyone to go outside except me.

Glenn Flack walked by and said, "You're in trouble, Mendal Dawes." Carol Anderson, who was my third-grade girlfriend, looked like she was going to cry, as if I'd written the letter to Ms. Suber myself.

Ms. Suber said, "You've done nothing wrong, Mendal. Please tell your daddy that I got it. When he asks what happened today, just say that Ms. Suber got it, okay?"

I put the letter in my front pants pocket. I said, "My father's a widower."

My father was waiting for me when I got home. Like everyone else, he started off in textiles, then gave it up. I never really knew what he did for a living, outside of driving around within a hundred-mile radius of Forty-Five buying up land and then reselling it when the time was right. He had a Knack. That was his word. For a time I thought it was the make of his car. "I drive around all day and buy land," he said more than once, before and after my mother took off to replace Patsy Cline. "I have a Knack."

I came home wearing my book bag, filled with math homework and an abacus. I said, "Hey, Dad."

He held his arms wide open, as if I were a returning P.O.W. "Did your teacher send back a note?"

I reached in my pocket and pulled out the letter from Heloise to Abelard. I handed it to him and said, "She made me quit reading."

"She made you quit reading? How far along did you get?"

I told him how I only got to the part about sugar-booger baby. I said, "Is this one of those lessons in life you keep telling me about, like when we went camping?" My father taught me early on how to tell the difference between regular leaves and poison ivy, the year before, when we camped out beside the Saluda River, far from any commode, waiting for him to gain a vision on which tract would be most saleable later.

"Goddamn it to hell. She didn't say anything else after you read the letter?"

My father wore a seersucker suit. He wore a string tie. I said, "She called recess pretty much in the middle of me reading the thing. This is some kind of practical joke, isn't it?"

My father looked at me as if I'd peed on his wing tips. He said, "Now why would I do something like that to the only human being I love in this world?"

I couldn't imagine why. Why would a man who—as he liked to tell me often—before my birth played baseball for the Yankees in the summer, football for the Packers in the winter, and competed in the Olympics, ever revert to playing jokes on a nine-year-old son of his? "Ms. Suber seemed kind of mad."

"Did she cry? Did she start crying? Did she turn her head away from y'all and blow her nose into a handkerchief? Don't hold back, Mendal. Don't think that you're embarrassing your teacher or anything for telling the truth. Ms. Suber would want you to tell the truth, wouldn't she?"

I said, "Uh-huh. Probably."

"Uh-huh probably she cried, or uh-huh probably she'd want you to tell the truth?" My father walked to the kitchen backward, pulled a bottle of bourbon from the shelf, and drank from it straight. Twenty years later on I would do the same thing, but over a dog that needed to be put to sleep.

I said, "Uh-huh. I told her you were a widower and everything. We got to go to recess early."

My father kept walking backward. He took a glass from the cabinet, then cracked open an ice tray. He put cubes in the glass, poured bourbon into it, and stood staring at me as if I had told secrets to the enemy. "Did she say that she's thinking about getting married?"

I said, "She didn't say anything."

I wondered if my mother stood before a group of men and women drinking house beer, if she sang "I Fall to Pieces" or "Crazy" or any of those other country songs. It wasn't but three thirty in my father's house. There was a one-hour time change, at least, in Nashville.

"I've gotten ahold of a genuine Cherokee Indian bracelet and ring," my father said the next Thursday night. "I ain't shitting you any on this one. Your mother's father gave them to us a long time ago as a wedding present. He got them when he was traveling through Cherokee County up in the Cherokee country. Your grandfather used to sell cotton, you know. Sometimes those Indians needed cotton. They traded things for cotton. That's the way things go."

I said, "I was thinking about taking some pinecones I found." I had gathered up some pinecones that were so perfect it wasn't funny. They looked like Christmas trees built to scale. "I was going to take a rock and say it was a meteorite."

"No, no. Take some of my Cherokee Indian jewelry, son. I don't mind. I don't care! Hotdamn I didn't even remember having the things, so it won't matter none if they get broken or stolen," he said. "This is the real thing, Bubba."

What could I do? I wasn't but nine years old, and early on I'd been taught to do whatever my elders said, outside of drinking whiskey and smoking cigarettes when they got drunk and made the offer, usually at Sunken Gardens Lounge. I thought, maybe

I can pretend to take my father's weird jewelry and stick it in my desktop. Maybe I can stick a pinecone inside my lunch box. "Yessir."

"I won't have it any other way," he said. "Wait here."

My father went back to what used to be my mother's and his bedroom. He opened up a wooden box he'd fashioned in high school shop, and pulled out a thin silver bracelet, plus a one-pearl ring. I didn't know that these trinkets once adorned the left arm of my third-grade teacher, right before she broke up with my father in order to go to college, and long before she graduated, taught in some other school system for ten years, and then came back to her hometown.

I took the trinkets in a small cotton sack. My father told me that he'd come get me for lunch if I wanted him to, that I didn't need to pack a bologna sandwich and banana as always. I went to the refrigerator and made my own and then left through the back door.

Glenn Flack started off show-and-tell with an X-ray of his mother's ankle. She'd fallen off the front porch trying to run from bees—something the rest of us knew not to do, seeing as we'd learned how to act in one of the weekly filmstrips. I got called next and said, "I have some priceless Cherokee Indian artifacts to show y'all. The Cherokee Indians had a way with hammering and chiseling." My father had made me memorize this speech.

I showed my classmates what ended up being something bought at Rey's Jewelers. Ms. Suber said, "Let me take a look at that," and got up to take the bracelet from my hand. She peered at it and then held it at arm's length and said, "This looks like it says 'sterling' on the inside, Mendal. I believe you might've picked up the wrong Indian jewelry to bring to school."

"Indian giver, Indian giver, Indian giver!" Melissa Beasley yelled out. It wasn't a taboo term back then. This was a time, understand, before we all had to say Native American–head penny.

I said, "I just know what my dad told me. That's all I know." I took the bracelet from Ms. Suber, pulled out the ring, and stood there as if offering a Milk-Bone to a stray and skittish dog.

Ms. Suber said, "I've had enough of this," and told me to return to my desk. I put the pearl ring on my thumb and stuck the bracelet around the toe of my tennis shoe. Ms. Suber said, "Has your father gone insane lately, Mendal?"

It embarrassed me, certainly, and if she had said it twenty or thirty years later, I could've sued her for harassment, slander, and making me potentially agoraphobic. My desk was in the last row. Every student turned toward me except Shirley Ebo, the only Black girl in the entire school, four years prior to lawful integration. She looked forward, as always, ready to approach the music stand and explain her show-and-tell object, a face jug made by an old, old relative of hers named Dave the Slave.

I said, "My father has a Knack." Maybe I said nothing, really, but I thought about my father's Knack. I waited.

Ms. Suber sat back down. She looked at the ceiling and said, "I'm sorry, Mendal. I didn't mean to yell at you. Everyone go on to recess."

And so it continued for six weeks. I finally told my father that I couldn't undergo any more humiliation, that I would play hooky, that I would show up at school and say I had forgotten to bring my show-and-tell gimcrack. I said, "I'm only going to take these stupid things you keep telling me stories about if it brings in some money, Dad."

Not that I was ever a capitalist or anything, but I figured early on that show-and-tell would end up somehow hurting my penmanship or spelling grade, and that maybe I needed to start saving money in order to get a head start in life should I not get into college. My father said, "That sounds fair enough. How much will you charge me to take this old, dried Mayan wrist corsage and matching boutonniere?"

I said, "Five bucks each."

My father handed them over. If the goddamn school system had ever shown a worthwhile Friday filmstrip concerning inductive logic, I would've figured out back then that when Ms. Suber and my father had had their horrific and execrable high school breakup, my father had gone over to her house and gathered up everything he'd ever bestowed upon her, from birthday to Valentine's Day to special three-month anniversary and so on. He had gifts she'd given him, too, I supposed much later, though I doubted they were worthy of monogamy.

But I didn't know logic. I thought only that my father hated the school system, had no trust whatsoever in public education, and wanted to drive my teacher to a nervous breakdown in order to get her to quit. Or, I thought, it was his way of flirting—that since my mother had "died," he wanted to show a prospective second wife some of the more spectacular possessions he could offer a needful woman.

He said, "I can handle ten dollars a show-and-tell session, for two items. Remind me not to give you an hourglass. I don't want you charging me per grain of sand."

This was all by the first of October. By Christmas break I'd brought in cufflinks worn by Louis Quatorze, a fountain pen used by the fifty-six signers of the Declaration of Independence (my father tutored me on stressing "Independence" when I announced my cherished object to the class), a locket once owned by Elmer the glue inventor, thus explaining why the thing couldn't be opened, a pack of stale Viceroys that once belonged to the men who raised the American flag on Iwo Jima. I brought in more famous love letters, all on lined Blue Horse paper:

from Ginger Rogers to Fred Astaire, from Anne Hathaway to Shakespeare, from all of Henry VIII's wives to him. One letter, according to my dad, was from Plato to Socrates, though he said it wasn't the original, and that he'd gone to the trouble of learning Greek in order to translate the thing.

Ms. Suber became exasperated with each new disclosure. She moved from picking names at random or in alphabetical order to always choosing me last. My classmates voted me Most Popular, Most Likely to Succeed, and Third Grade President, essentially because I got us ten more minutes of recess every Friday.

I walked down to the County Bank every Friday after school and deposited the money my father had forked over in a regular savings account. This was a time before IRAs. It was a time before stock portfolios, mutual funds, and the like. They gave me a toaster for starting the account and a dinner plate every time I walked in with ten dollars or more. After a few months I could've hosted a dinner party for twelve.

On Saturday mornings, more often than not, I drove with my father from place to place, looking over land he had bought or planned to buy. He had acquired a few acres of woodland before my birth, and soon thereafter the Army Corps of Engineers came in, flooded the Savannah River, and made my father's property near lakefront. He sold that parcel, took that money, and bought more land in an area that bordered what would become I-95. He couldn't go wrong. My father was not unlike the fool who threw darts at a map and went with his gut instinct. He would buy useless swampland, and someone else would soon insist on buying that land at twice to ten times his cost in order to build a golf course, a subdivision, or a nuclear-power facility. I had no idea what he did between these ventures, outside of reading and wondering. How else would he know about Abelard and Heloise, or even Socrates and Plato? He hadn't gone to college. He hadn't taken some kind of correspondence course.

We drove, and I stuck my head out the window like the dog I had owned before my mother took him to Nashville. We'd get to some land, pull down a dirt road usually, and my father would stare hard for ten or fifteen minutes. He barely turned his head from side to side, and he never turned off the engine. Sometimes he'd say at the end, "I think I got a fouled spark plug," or "You can tell that that gas additive's working properly."

He never mentioned people from history, or the jewelry of the dead. I took along Hardy Boys mysteries but never opened the covers. Finally, one afternoon, I said, "Ms. Suber wants to know if you're planning on coming to the PTA meeting. I forgot to tell you."

My father turned off the ignition. He reached beneath his seat and pulled out a can of beer and a church key. We sat parked between two gullies, somewhere in Greenwood County. "Hotdamn, boy, you need to tell me these things. When is it?"

I said, "I forgot. I got in so much trouble Friday that I forgot." I'd taken a tortoise to show-and-tell and said his name was John the Baptist. At first Ms. Suber seemed delighted. When she asked why I had named him John the Baptist, I said, "Watch this." I screamed, "John the Baptist!" When he retreated into his shell and lost his head, I nodded. She had me sit back down. None of my classmates got the joke.

"The PTA meeting's on Tuesday. It's Tuesday." I wore a pair of cut-off blue jeans with the bottoms cut into one-inch strips. My mother used to make them for me when I'd grown taller but hadn't gained weight around the middle. I had on my light-blue Little League T-shirt, with Sunken Gardens on the front and 69 for my number on the back. My father had insisted that I get that number, and that I would thank him one day.

"Hell, yes. Do I need to bring anything? I mean, is this one of those meetings where parents need to bring food? I know how to make potato salad. I can make potato salad and coleslaw, you know."

"She just asked me to ask if you'd show up. That's all she said, I swear."

My father looked out at what I understood to be another wasteland. Empty beer cans were scattered in front of us, and the remains of a haphazard bonfire someone had made right in the middle of a path. "Maybe I should call her up and ask if she needs anything."

Although I didn't understand the depth of my father's obsession, I said, "Ms. Suber won't be in town until that night. We have a substitute on Monday, 'cause she has to go to a funeral somewhere."

My father drank from his beer. He handed the can over and told me to take little sips at first. I said, "Mom wouldn't want you to give me beer."

He nodded. "Mom wouldn't want you to do a lot of things, just like she didn't want me to do a lot of things. But she's not here, is she? Your momma's spending all her time praying that she never gets laryngitis, while the rest of us hope she does."

I didn't know that my father had been taking Fridays off in order to see the school secretary, feign needing to leave me a bag lunch, and then stand looking through the vertical window of my classroom door while I expounded on the rarity of a letter sweater once worn by General Custer, or whatever. When the PTA meeting came around, I went with my father, though no other students attended. Pretty much it was only parents, teachers, and a couple of the lunch ladies who had volunteered to serve a punch of ginger ale and grape juice. My father entered

Ms. Suber's classroom and approached her as if she were a newspaper boy he'd forgotten to pay. He said, "I thought you'd eventually send a letter home asking for a conference. I thought you'd finally buckle under." To me he said, "Go look at the goldfish, Mendal. You've always liked aquariums. Maybe I'll get you one."

I looked at the corner of the room. My classmates' parents were sitting at tiny desks, their knees bobbing like the shells of surfaced turtles. My third-grade teacher said, "I know you think this is cute, but it's not. I don't know why you think you can recourt me however many years later after what you did to me back then."

My father pushed me in the direction of the aquarium. Ms. Suber waved and smiled at Glenn Flack's parents, who were walking in. I said, "Can I go sit in the car?"

Ms. Suber said, "You stay right here, Mendal."

"I might not have been able to go to college like you did, Lola, but I've done good for myself," my father said. I thought one thing only: *Lola?*

"I know you have, Lee. I know you've done well. And let me be the first to say how proud I am of you, and how I'm sorry if I hurt you, and that I've seen you looking in the window when Mendal does his bogus show-and-tells." She pointed at the window in the door. Mr. and Mrs. Anderson walked in. "I need to start this thing up."

My father said to me, "If you want to go sit in the car, go ahead." He handed me the keys, leaned down, and said, "There's a beer in the glove compartment, son."

Let me say that this was South Carolina in 1968. Although my memory's not perfect, I think that at the time, neither drinking nor driving was against the law for minors, nor was smoking cigarettes before the age of twelve. Five years later I would drive my mini-bike to the Sunken Gardens, meet one of the Black boys twirling trays out in the parking lot, order my eight-pack of Miller ponies, and have it delivered to me without conscience or threat of law.

I pretended to go into the parking lot but circled around to the outside of Ms. Suber's classroom. I stood beneath one of the six jalousies, crouched, and listened. Ms. Suber welcomed the parents and said that it was an exciting year. She said something about how all of us would have to take a national test later on to see how we compared with the rest of the nation. She said something about a school play. Ms. Suber warned parents of a looming head-lice epidemic. She paced back and forth and asked everyone to introduce himself or herself. Someone asked if the school would ever sponsor another cake-and-pie sale in order to buy new recorders. My father said he'd be glad to have a potato-salad-and-cole-slaw sale. I didn't hear the teacher's answer. From where I crouched I could only look up at the sky and notice how some stars twinkled madly while others shone hard and fast like mica afire.

By the time I reached high school, my mother had moved from Nashville to New Orleans and then from New Orleans to Las Vegas. She never made it as a country singer or a blues singer, but she seemed to thrive as a hostess of sorts. As I crouched there beneath a window jutting out above boxwoods, I thought of my mother and imagined what she might be doing at the moment my father was experiencing his first PTA meeting. Was she crooning to conventioneers? Was she sitting in a back room worrying over pantyhose? That's what I thought, I swear to God. Everyone in Ms. Suber's classroom seemed to be talking with cookies in their mouths. I heard my father laugh hard twice—once when Ms. Suber said she knew that her students saw her as a witch, and another time when she said she knew that her students went home complaining that she didn't spank exactly the way their parents spanked.

Again, this was in the middle of the Vietnam War. Spanking made for good soldiers.

My third-grade teacher said that she didn't have anything else to say, and told her students' parents to feel free to call her up should they have questions concerning grades, expectations, or field trips. She said she appreciated anyone who wanted to help chaperone kids or work after school in a tutoring capacity. I stood up and watched my friends' parents leave single file, my father last in line.

Fifteen minutes after I'd gotten back in the car, five minutes after everyone else had driven out of the parking lot, I climbed out the passenger side and crept back to Ms. Suber's window. I expected my father to have Lola Suber in a headlock, or backed up against the Famous Christians of the World corkboard display. I didn't foresee their having moved desks against the walls in order to make a better dance floor.

My father held my third-grade teacher in a way I'd seen him hold a woman only once before: one Fourth of July he had danced with my mother in the backyard while the neighbors shot bottle rockets straight up. My mother had placed her head on his shoulder and smiled, her eyes raised to the sky. Lola Suber didn't look upward. She didn't smile either. My father seemed to be humming, or talking low. I couldn't hear exactly what went on, but years later he confessed that he had set forth everything he meant to say and do, everything he hoped she taught the other students and me when it came to matters of passion.

I did hear Lola Suber remind him that they had broken up because she had decided to have a serious and exclusive relationship with Jesus Christ.

There amid the boxwoods I hunkered down and thought

only about the troubles I might have during future show-and-tells. I stood back up, saw them dancing, and returned to the car. I would let my father open the glove compartment later. ⊙

Imagine explosions here

Christine McSwain

I was thirteen that summer with knees peeled raw like split peaches, bony elbows sharper than my sense of self, and a dead mom no one wanted to talk about.

Dad sat my brother and me down at the kitchen table one night, his fingers drumming a rhythm against a fat white envelope. I figured it was another one of Mom's hospital bills, the exhausting type that listed each charge down to a single Band-Aid, reminding us of every administered poke and prod.

Ethan, seven years old and red-faced from a mosquito bite on his cheek that he would not stop scratching, sat across from me. He kicked his chair legs and made little wounded animal sounds like he was daring me to shut him up. Neither of us looked at the envelope long enough to notice the glimpse of a logo in the top corner, and even if we had, the majority of it was obscured by Dad's skillfully placed thumb and index finger. He took his place at the table on my right side, flipped the envelope over, and peeled it open, slow and obnoxious, savoring the reveal. Out came a big, glossy folder in screaming blue, the logo a globe in repose—Universal Studios. Among the pamphlets inside was one for the *Jaws* ride, based on the movie I'd seen once. In fierce yellow letters: *ATTACKING SUMMER 1990*.

Mom died the year before. Uterine cancer—quick and mean. I had heard funeral-goers say that it was better for her that way, to have not suffered for so long. I knew better.

Dad didn't want us to spend her first death anniversary at her grave as we had done each month since she died, standing in the sun, taking turns clearing our throats to fill the awkward silence. Instead, he'd decided to take us down to Orlando for a weekend of heat and noise. I imagined him booking the trip in late-night phone calls, muttering price points behind the kitchen wall, hushed and giddy.

Mom was the daredevil among us. Nothing scared her—she rode roller coasters no-handed and laughed through her teeth at every drop. She thought Disney was too tame, too polished for a woman who loved to feel her heart slamming against her ribs. When she died, I was meant to inherit the role. She left me her fearlessness, but I hadn't learned to wear it yet. Truth be told, the big rides scared me, and being suspended upside down made me retch. But just about anything was better than staring at that new rectangle of grass above Mom, a sign that the ground had already devoured her, wondering how long it would take to settle as if it had never been dug.

"Pass it on," Ethan whined. "Vail, let me see it!"

I couldn't take my eyes off the dead-eyed leviathan on the page. Its teeth came out of its mouth every which way, sharp like the kitchen knives I was finally allowed to touch. Ethan tugged at the pamphlet in my hand, his bellyaching needling into my skull—*let me see it, let me see it, let me see it.* He wrenched it from my hands and left the edge damaged, making the shark's nose deformed and wrong-looking. I watched my little brother's eyes dart back and forth in that minuscule, chaotic way—the same as they did behind his closed eyelids when I knew he was dreaming. He stared hard at the shark on the slick, loud paper, then looked back at me.

"Is it real?" Ethan had that hitch in his voice that he got when entertaining irrational fears. Not quite the precursor to a real cry, but the staccato inhale from a round of hysterics bubbling up inside.

Our elderly chihuahua, Gus, moseyed to his empty food bowl in the corner of the kitchen. The clicks of his unclipped nails against the linoleum came in couplets that quickened as he got closer to us. Dad tapped a finger on the table and then pointed to the cabinet underneath the sink.

"Feed the beast," he told me, then turned to Ethan. "It's as real as you want it to be."

According to the sign outside the boathouse, we'd be in line for at least an hour. Jaws was still new, famous for frequent malfunctions. I'd heard people in line wondering if there would be technical difficulties. I had a wild hope that we would get through the whole thing without a hitch in the machinery. The line moved forward into the shade, which meant the operators were gambling on the thing staying alive long enough to fake a few deaths. That was optimism theme park-style: Keep the bodies moving.

Ethan made a fuss about the waiting until Dad and I bribed him with an electric-blue Icee. We stood inside the boathouse with mist tickling our arms, keeping us cool as it mixed with a frigid artificial breeze. I took long sips from a water bottle as big as my head and glanced at Dad after every gulp.

"Rule number one: Don't get dehydrated," he'd told us in the hotel room the night before. Ethan was sprawled across the bed watching *The Simpsons*, not listening. "Drink water all day.

I don't care how many times you gotta hit the bathroom. I'd rather deal with a grody theme park toilet than scrape one of you off the pavement."

He never told us the second rule.

Ethan sucked the Icee down too fast and suffered an inevitable brain freeze. He wanted to go sit down, he said. Dad clicked his tongue.

"Put your tongue on the roof of your mouth and suck on it," Dad said. I was skeptical. Ethan's jaw lowered, and I could see the purple, veined underside of his tongue as he pulled the brain freeze right out, relief melting over him.

Dad couldn't keep our white socks truly white, and he couldn't fold a fitted sheet to save his life, but I'd be damned if he wasn't some kind of wizard. He had a quick fix for everything. I'd never seen Dad cry. Even at the funeral, he had the ghost of a grin in his mouth. We sat on the front row of pews in front of Mom's powder-blue casket. I wished that it had been black so that maybe I could study my reflection in it, so I could see my face enough to untwist it and feel as serene as Dad had looked. How did he do it? How did he make himself a dam, right there in his chest?

I could see our boat coming up on the noxious green-blue water, our skipper waving us on. His name tag said "Beau," and he was probably eighteen—maybe even a college student—which truly thrilled me. He had big, dark eyes and a tasteful mullet that grazed the back of his sun-pinked neck. He was just about the prettiest thing I'd ever seen. I braced myself as he helped the people in front of us board, his tanned hands gripping wrist after wrist, his voice all smooth as if he was the prince of that man-made lagoon. He helped Ethan onto the boat with ease. Then it was my turn.

"Watch your step, honey," he warned. "Skipper's gotta keep the ladies safe."

I swooned—heady with infatuation, deep with the kind of obsession that felt urgent and ridiculous. I put my hand in Beau's (what a name!) and squeezed, feeling the way his fingers closed around mine without hesitation. I stepped aboard, still drunk on the hand-holding. Then Dad scooted between Ethan and me and threw his arm around my shoulder.

"I'm scared, Vail! I don't think he knows what he's doing." He liked to think he was funny. At that moment, he was not.

"Are you a real sailor?" Ethan asked. Beau was a skipper, not a sailor. I knew this because I listened. I felt insulted on Beau's behalf, but he wasn't bothered.

"I'm as real as they come," he said, grinning with a quip on his tongue like he'd been asked many times before. "Are you a real little boy?"

Mom had just gotten around to talking to me about boys before she died. I'd been growing restless in my regular English class. I finished the required novels too fast, scrawling margin notes while everyone else was still decoding metaphors. I'd started reading ahead, then reading sideways, until the teacher said I needed more room to stretch. So they sent me down the road in the afternoons to observe the ninth-grade English class, where I sat in the back and tried not to look younger than I was.

I'd had a crush on Orion Fletcher—an impressive-to-me fifteen-year-old with a pale, serious face and a mouth made for arguing. He had a kind of sincerity that made everything he said sound urgent, especially when he talked about the women missing from the syllabus. As if their absence were a personal affront. My heart had stuttered like a bird hitting glass when he said, "We'd be nothing without the woman's voice, Mr. Howell."

I came home that day to tell Mom I had fallen in love. She was peeling an orange with slow, deliberate fingers like she was trying not to bruise it. The peel came off in one long, fragile ribbon across her lap. The fruit sat half undone in her palm, wet and shining.

"The boy being named after a constellation doesn't mean he's worth studying," she'd said, then laughed. She didn't look up. Her hands kept moving, gentle and careful like she was holding something she knew wouldn't last.

Beau pointed out the New England houses crouched along the shore as if he'd grown up in one of them. He told us about the people who'd lived there—their quiet lives and their violent deaths, about the ones who fought and the ones who ran. He spoke with the smooth confidence of someone who had been there, and I almost believed him. Never mind that I had already found the truth. I had traced the inked letters of Peter Benchley's name with my own fingers in the fiction section of the library. Beau wasn't fooling me, except that he was. As far as I was concerned, I was in a doomed vessel off the coast of Amity, the wind salt-thick in my hair and the ocean wild and waiting. As damned as I was, I felt at peace.

"How many of you have seen the movie *Jaws*?" I raised my hand, as did everyone else in the boat. Beau nodded, and I knew it was a bold-faced lie because Ethan was unconscious in the next room over, breathing deep and easy, that night Mom and I stayed up so late.

Dad leaned in and whispered, "When the hell did you watch *Jaws*?"

"I watched it with Mom," I answered, then shushed him.

"Well, luckily, you all just saw the film," Beau said. He was deep in the script, voice laced with showmanship as he strung me along. "We had to live through that."

Mayday. Mayday. Is anybody out there? Help! Help!

The desperate voice, swallowed by frantic static, came from Beau's headset. He staggered back and clutched his hand over his heart. I looked at Ethan. He sat stiff-backed, his eyes darting left to right as if he could see something circling beneath us. Dad threw an arm around him, easy and loose, grinning at the chlorine like he was watching a magic trick, not staring down a certain death by jagged teeth and bleeding gums.

"Amity 6 to base, did you copy that transmission?" Beau held the microphone of his headset to his lips so closely he nearly kissed it. "It sounded like it was Gordon over on Amity 3. Over."

I watched him fill with dread, then wrestle it back down—all for us, all for the sake of the show. For a moment, I thought I saw his bottom lip tremble. What a performance. What a star.

Ten-four, we copied. Can't be too far away—he was headed back in. We could hear every word from Beau's headset. *We're picking up his distress signal now. Keep an eye out for him. I'll call Chief Brody. Base clear.* The radio cut out with a sizzle.

Beau rounded a corner and flung out an arm, pointing to the left.

"Oh no," he breathed. We turned just in time to see it—a boat identical to ours, tilted upright in the water, its bow jutting skyward as it bobbed once, twice, then vanished, sucked down like something had dragged it under. The jewel-toned water rippled. Then, a fin. It cut through the surface, sleek and deliberate, moving toward us.

Behind me cried a chorus of screams: "Shark!"

Beau spun back, his hands a blur as he reached for the grenade launcher bolted to the boat's console. He threw it against his shoulder and fired, the hollow *pop! pop!* breaking out over the water.

"Missed! Missed again!" he announced, his voice pitched for panic. He yanked the wheel and pulled us hard into a second boathouse. The doors creaked shut behind us and sealed us inside. We were in total darkness except for the single headlight mounted to the front of the boat. Beau swiveled it toward the water, and the beam caught me in the face, making it impossible to see anything beyond its reach.

"Did anyone hear that?"

The mechanical shark surfaced and lunged at the opposite side of the boat. I could barely see the shape of its snout in the darkness before it submerged again. It made no sound. It didn't need to—the screams of other passengers rang through the boathouse.

The lights came on and Beau pulled us forward, out into the open water. Beau pressed his headset against his ear for another transmission: *Amity 6, this is Chief Brody. I'll be there in ten minutes.*

"Oh, ten minutes!" Beau wailed, then reached for the grenade launcher like he wouldn't miss this time. "We're gonna be shark bait in ten minutes!"

On Mom's dark days, I would ask her to tell me the story of my name.

"You were conceived in Vail, Colorado, on our honeymoon," she'd say, lips dry but smiling. "Something, something. A joke about not wasting time. You already know."

"I like it better when you say it." I shrugged and crunched the ice chips the nurse brought for Mom, which she shared with me. She didn't know how to not give me everything she had.

She'd shaved her head before the chemo could claim her hair, leaving behind pieces of a buzz cut—tiny continents adrift on the translucent ocean of her skull. I looked at her head like I was watching a planet from the International Space Station.

"Your dad knows it just as good as I do," she whispered, not bothering to open her eyes. "He was there too. Obviously."

Dad was down in the cafeteria with Ethan, probably pretending that a sad scoop of vanilla ice cream with a careless drizzle of hot fudge on top was a real treat.

"Please," I said. She didn't answer.

Some days, even though I knew she was just sleeping and her body needed more rest than it could hold, I would slip the compact mirror from my jacket pocket and angle it under her nose. I'd seen it in a movie once: a trick to prove life with a fogged glass.

"I'm not dead yet," she'd said. Her eyes didn't open. "You'll know when it's for real."

In a cyclone of chlorine and whirring gears, the shark breached the water on my side of the boat, his sharp, wrong teeth glaring in the sun. I felt my throat tighten, so I shut my eyes. I braced for the splash, for the shift of water beneath us, for the screams—but all I caught was Ethan's, high and ragged, cutting through the rest.

Then silence. A mechanical click, then nothing. The shark stayed in place, its mouth hanging open as water dripped down its gray hide. I could look into its left eye, a black orb that didn't blink or glint. The whole boat stopped and rocked once, then settled.

Beau aimed his grenade launcher at the gas canister behind the shark, the click of the trigger all the more pathetic now that everything had come to a halt. Ethan stood up to give the shark a cautious, closer look. Beau didn't stop him.

"What's wrong with it?" He looked at me, wide-eyed but quiet. Dad gently but firmly pulled Ethan back to his seat, and then touched my arm.

"You okay?" he asked. I said I was, but I couldn't stop looking at the shark. Its black eye could fit into the palm of my hand.

Beau must have been nervous being stuck with a disillusioned crowd on an immovable boat—he gestured at the gas cans he'd pretended to shoot. His mouth made weak *pew pew* noises, then a sloppy, wet imitation of a blast. *Pfoom!* Spittle burst from his lips in a thin arc, flecking his chin. He didn't wipe it off. It was gross. He let out a long sigh through his nose then lifted both hands to make one more lazy, half-assed *BOOM* motion, fingers splayed like fire blooming from the sky. He held it for a beat too long, then let his arms fall to his sides like deadweight.

"Imagine explosions here."

Mom died at home. Hospice had been kind enough to set her up in the living room so we could watch TV together while the cancer ate her up from the inside. Ethan was allowed a TV in his room so he could avoid Mom altogether. He tried not to be, but he was afraid of her—the last little bit of her still holding on. He was too young to see her lying there, swallowed up by the blue-and-purple afghan she knit during her last Christmas. My brother and I would keep growing up after Mom was dead, and one day, we would be people she never knew.

That night, after *Cheers*, I stayed curled on the couch behind her bed. The next program started—a girl diving into the ocean, a song sung by flutes leading her in. It was hard to tell if she was naked or not. I watched through the metal bars of Mom's hospital bed, the lines of her body between me and the flickering light.

I must have dozed off. When I woke up, a man I didn't know was on the screen, maneuvering around in a quickly sinking boat turned sideways. I sat up just in time to see it—the shark, huge and furious, crashed through the hull, its mouth bursting open like a wound. Its teeth were strung with red-pink meat, ribbons of something once living.

I looked over at Mom so we could laugh at the way I'd jumped at the sound of the shark's attack. I remember her eyes were barely opened, her lips parted slightly. I put my hand on her shoulder and felt nothing inside of her—no movement, no rattling. I knew.

On the screen, the boat exploded—red and white against the blue, a victory too loud, too late. The air in the room felt crowded and hollow all at once. Still full of us, but she was gone.

Mom had told us not to be sad for long.

"The world won't stop to let you off," she'd told us.

I didn't care what she said.

The water stained red. I lay back down on the couch, arms crossed and pressed close to my chest, and I closed my eyes. I would wake Dad up and tell him, but not yet.

I used to hate the water, one voice on the TV said.

A different one laughed.

I can't imagine why.

We finally moved along the track that kept us on the shark's stalking path. The other mechanical sharks were at rest, defunct robots stilled underneath chemical-laden water. Before we returned to the start, I could see the tip of a nose below the surface, its teeth lined in a blurry white row, frozen perpetually in its scripted attack.

Beau jumped off the boat when we got to the dock, leaving us to disembark ourselves. Dad gave Ethan a boost onto land, climbed out, and then offered his hand to me. I took it and kept my eyes on Beau as I got out. His back was turned when he took his headset off and said to the other skippers, in a voice not meant for my ears, "Fuck that shark."

We walked back through the boathouse and out into the humidity. I'd expected Ethan to go into one of his deep-breath tantrums—the ones where he gulped air so quickly that he gave himself the hiccups. He looked serene. A little red in the face from the heat, but calm.

Dad was quiet. I looked up at him. He was so much taller than me. The sun sat directly behind the brim of his cap, turning his whole head into an eclipse. I couldn't make out his face, but I knew he was crying.

Mom had rules, too—not written down, not said. They were rules she lived by and entered my bloodstream and stayed there.

The first was no crying. The second was that if something scares you, do it anyway.

I took the half-warm water bottle Dad tucked into the pocket of his cargo shorts. I drank until I was plump with water, like I was water, too. The plastic crinkled in my grip. I drank until it hurt—until my stomach felt heavy and slow and real.

Dad had broken the first rule, not his but mom's. I wouldn't break Dad's rule. The water sloshed against the walls of me, knocking at my ribs like it wanted out. I hoped the dam I built would hold it back. ⊙

Nothing for the Journey

Andrew Siegrist

The boy's hands smelled like asphalt and the girl held them tight like she was afraid if the world kept spinning she'd lose her balance.

He'd hung their shoes from a trestle bridge and left them dangling above the water. They both walked slow in the dew-wet grass beside a road neither of them had ever been on before.

The boy took coins and acorn caps from his pockets and flicked them into the ditch, because you can't take nothing for the journey, he said. When he wasn't looking, the girl picked up a Mercury dime and closed it tight in her fist.

She didn't know his name. He had green eyes the color of a memory she couldn't place, and blond hair cut short and uneven, like he'd done it himself in a room without mirrors. He spoke slow and smiled shy when he looked at her. She worried if he knew anything about her at all that smile would turn. That brightness in his eyes would dull and he'd see her the same way everyone else did.

So when he asked questions, she lied. Told him her skin was dark from Indian blood. Told him when she was in high school, she ran away from home and lived with her grandmother on a reservation in the mountains of North Carolina. Said she could braid bird feathers into patterns that would show the future, and that her grandmother gave her nicknames like Smooth Stone, Little Mouse, and Bone.

They ate breakfast in a diner before the sun came up. She had the word of the Lord tattooed across the back of her neck, and the boy traced each letter with his pinky finger and swore her skin was warmer there somehow. The girl scooted close to him and rested her head against his chest so she could feel the vibrations of his voice.

Tell me one true thing, she said. One thing you never told anyone, so it'll be just me and you that know it.

The boy's first pet was an imaginary friend named Pumpernickel. Pumpernickel was a sheepdog, had eyes two different colors, and would bark out small sentences the boy could understand when he was alone.

Pumpernickel was hit by a car on the boy's fifth birthday and was buried in the shade of a hemlock tree.

Never told anyone that? she said.

Promise, he said.

Cross your heart, she said. Hope to die.

He kissed her on the top of her head. It was summer and in summer her hair always smelled like rain. She put her head in his lap and stretched her legs across the vinyl booth. There was a scar running up her ankle and he asked for the story.

The truth? she said.

And he waited.

She'd been pregnant the night she saw lightning and snow at the same time. Her dad called it Coldthunder, and she walked out into it and listened to so much quiet be broken by the crack of strange, electric-blue light. The snow was thick on the ground and she climbed a tree to the high branches to see above it all. Didn't realize her hands had gone numb until she tried to climb down and lost her grip. Her dad laid her in the back of the car and drove to the hospital with her crooked leg raised on a stack of pillows. And that's where they learned about the baby. The doctors said if it had survived, she wouldn't have started showing for a couple weeks. Her dad said it was for the best, that she was only a child herself. On the drive home, the lightning had stopped and all around was a covering of white beneath dark sky.

The boy wasn't smiling, but that brightness was still in his eyes and, for a moment, the girl let herself believe he'd never looked at anyone like that before.

Does it still hurt? the boy said.

She covered the scar on her ankle with a napkin.

When bone breaks, she said, it grows stronger where it heals. Strong as iron.

The check came. She unfastened her necklace and laid it on the table. The necklace was silver. The shape of a feather.

He followed her outside and they watched through the window as the waitress put the necklace around her neck. Then they crossed the street to the bus station. He didn't ask where she was going.

She didn't tell him she was going home, that she'd called her father the night before for the first time in two years.

She stepped into the bus, squeezed down the aisle and into a seat by the window.

He stood outside and tossed parking-lot gravel at the bus until she looked out.

Your name, he said. Your name.

When she spoke, her breath fogged the glass and he couldn't read her lips. She waited until the bus was far away. She traced her name through the cloud her breath had left against the window. A child stood on the seat in front of her and rested his chin on the seat back. She felt in her pocket for the Mercury dime she'd saved that morning. She handed the child the coin. The child put it in his mouth and raised a finger to his lips. She smiled and wiped the fog from the window. Nothing for the journey. Not even her own name.

Years later, when the boy dreamed, she'd be there walking the dew grass or sitting in a diner with her head against his chest. He would call her Smooth Stone or Little Mouse, and she would scatter bird feathers on the table, arranging them so that the future was something they didn't have to fear. And when he was awake, he'd watch for her, imagining her in front of him in line at the checkout counter in a grocery store somewhere. Or moving outside his kitchen window, tapping the glass, as if meeting that way was something they had planned. Her hair would be longer, but still the smell of rain. And he would know to call her Bone. Bone, broken then healed. Bone so much stronger than iron. ⊙

THE PICKERS

Michel Stone

The pickers show up in late May, right before school lets out, near your birthday. The dirt road to your house splits piney woods from the fields, so any time you go someplace or come back you pass them, bent among the rows like living scarecrows, the hard, green tomatoes thundering into their buckets. You like the way the air smells this time of year, like thunderstorms and blossoms, the way the holly bushes vibrate with bees, and inchworms dangle from who knows where.

Mama tells you the pickers are mostly Mexicans but may be also from other places like Honduras or Guatemala, and they travel wherever crops need gathering. That's what *migrant* means, she says. They have children out there with them and you think how weird and magical those kids' lives must be, travelling from place to place like that. You've never been out of South Carolina, except one time when your family went up to the Blue Ridge Parkway in North Carolina. That was last summer, when you were eight.

You still think about those mountains and how, on the way back home to the Lowcountry, you faced backward in the station wagon, believing if you never took your eyes off those smoky peaks, you could see them forever. You ended up accidentally falling asleep and when you woke up somewhere around Columbia the mountains were gone.

Anyway, you're curious about where those migrant children attend school. You ask Mama. She's not sure. She tells you they speak Spanish. You wonder what that'd be like, talking a different language in a faraway country and getting to be outside all day while the kids who live there are stuck in school.

You wish you could be friends with a migrant child, but no one knows any of them except for Mr. Jenkins, the farmer who owns the tomato fields. Coming home from school one afternoon, you see him driving out of the field in his pickup. Mama pulls over so they can get by one another. When she does this, you get a good, long look at the pickers. You see a little girl about your age squatting at a nearby row, dropping tomatoes into a red, plastic bucket, like all the other red, plastic buckets the pickers use. You stare at her hard, thinking if you look at her long enough, begging her in your mind to look up at you, she will. In a way, it's like when you wanted to keep looking at those Blue Ridge Mountains last summer, like your eyes could make the thing they saw do what you wanted. Anyway, Mama has lowered her window and she and Mr. Jenkins say *hey* and Mama says *how's tomato season going* and he says *really need some rain it's getting too dry* and just when Mama is saying *it's hottern' Hades*, the girl in the field looks right at you. Your heart thumps and you wave at her, quickly, before she can look away.

She wears a pink shirt and a floppy straw hat but you can see her eyes, big and brown. She smiles wide, not shy at all like you figure you'd be if you were in her country and a Mexican stranger waved at you from her mama's car on the side of a road. Mama is already driving again. You and that girl stare at each other until the sandy dirt from the tires rises and blocks her from view. You think of that dust powdering her hair and clothes and that she's probably sweaty. You wonder where she'll take a bath tonight, where she'll sleep, and what her name is. You wonder what she'll eat for supper. You ask Mama how to say your name in Mexican. She says, *You mean in Spanish*? You say, *Yes m'am, Spanish*. She says, *Well… Elizabeth is Elizabeth. I think your name is your name no matter where you say it.*

You search the field for the girl's floppy hat and pink shirt every time you pass until the migrants leave in late June, but you never see her again. How she looked at you as long as you looked at her makes you know, in the way only nine-year-old girls can know, that she was thinking about being your friend as much as you wanted to be hers.

One especially hot Friday after school, not too long after you saw the girl in the pink shirt, but before summer vacation, you hear sirens when you're out in your yard playing with your dog Mud. His name is Mud because you and your little brothers found him wandering in the marsh and pluff mud in front of your house last Thanksgiving break. It was low tide. You bogged out there, careful to avoid the oyster beds, and grabbed him while Pete and Jackie Boy cheered you on from the dock where they sat dangling their feet. You set the mud-caked puppy down in the grass, and he didn't mind when you and your brothers cleaned him under the hose. He was just the sweetest, little yellow dog and you and your brothers loved him then. Y'all begged Mama and Daddy to let you keep him, and they finally said yes.

Mama said, *Wonder where on earth he wandered up from,* and Daddy said, *Somebody probably tossed him from the bridge, not wanting another pet to feed.*

In your head you see what Daddy said happening like a TV

show and you picture the face of the person who could throw a live dog off a bridge. That person would be creepy, with ugly eyes that made everyone want to turn away from him. The thought gives you the shivers.

Anyway, you hear the *WEE-ow WEE-ow WEE-ow* of a siren far away and you and Mud walk down to the riverbank because the sound seems to be coming from across the river.

You look toward the bridge that joins Johns Island, where you live, to Wadmalaw Island, and you see a whole mess of emergency vehicles, lights flashing. You're sticky-sweaty, the hot air feels heavy as steam, but the lights blinking make you think of Christmastime, which is weird because the world smells of gardenias and mowed grass and salt marsh, not at all Christmassy.

You walk to the end of the dock because that gives you a better view of the bridge and you sit down, careful not to get splinters in your legs. Mud sits beside you and sniffs the seagull poop splattered on the dock like dried white paint and you watch the activity at the bridge, guessing what might have brought those ambulances plus a fire truck, even when there's no smoke or flames. Those emergency lights make your insides feel electric because something bad is unfolding down the river. You watch, thinking maybe the police caught the creepy man pitching puppies.

When Mama rings the bell on the porch, you know it's suppertime, so you go back to the house, but not before a police boat shows up under the bridge, and you think that's something you've never seen before: a police boat.

Mama says she heard somebody drowned, likely crabbing and went in too deep and got caught in the current. Daddy says the tide whips under that bridge pretty fast and could suck an unaware person right in. He teaches you and Pete and Jackie Boy the word *undertow* and says, *That's why you never go swimming someplace unfamiliar without a grown-up.* You and Pete say *yes sir*, and Jackie Boy just keeps gnawing on a cob of Silver Queen corn because he's four.

The next morning you skip watching cartoons and instead go out to the riverbank because you're kind of sad and feeling spooky but also eager to find out more about the person who got sucked into the river. You feel the goose bumps rise when you think about the body of a dead person that could be somewhere nearby, just under the surface of the river, *your* river, where you've splashed and fished and crabbed your whole life, the place where you found sweet Mud. Now, police boats are dragging the water with nets, and divers in strange suits with air tanks like Jacques Cousteau pop through the surface every now and then.

Around lunchtime, a man who works with Daddy stops by the house to drop off a chainsaw he's borrowed and you hear him say, "Aww, John, it was just one of them damn Mexican migrants drowned last evening." Daddy says something about that being a shame and that he hopes the fellow turns up soon. You wonder how the man returning the chainsaw knew the migrant was from Mexico and not from Honduras or Guatemala.

Just before suppertime, they find the migrant's body. He had drifted past your dock, because that's where the searchers found him, down river.

You feel weird inside, mixed up in a way you can't name. You think hard on that feeling for days, long after everyone else seems to have forgotten the drowning.

You look at the migrants in the fields and wonder if the drowned man had a child, and if he did, you wish you could have been friends with his daughter or son. You like to think maybe, somehow, you could have been helpful and kind if y'all were friends. You'd have said, *I'm so sorry about your daddy,* and you'd think about them being far from home. You wonder where they had a funeral, in South Carolina or back in Mexico or wherever the dead man came from. And if they buried him back in Mexico or wherever, how'd they get his body there.

That unnamed feeling never quite goes away and you think about the migrants every May around your birthday and sometimes you imagine meeting that girl in the floppy hat as a grown-up. You hope it wasn't her daddy who drifted past your house. You think of her big, brown eyes and her smile and you wish you knew her name. ⊙

Tennessee

Scott Gloden

I can't point to the moment in time my mother officially relinquished logic, but I can compare the instances: I can catalog crazy, as it were. Make no mistake, the candidacy of these occurrences, over a very short period, had become substantial. My mother robbed hardware stores, sexually assaulted a young man bagging her groceries, ate my father, and placed me in credit card debt. And, yes, that's the order I retell it—not based on the dramas that ensued, but in a chronology I am at least privy to owning.

Yet, in the backyard, the spade tip of the shovel half eaten in the dirt, and I can probably name what disappeared her for good.

My father was not my old man, but my very old man. My mother was over twenty years his junior, and by the time she had me, her only biological possession, she was already too old to be doing so. Of the situation, my uncle would often restate to me, once he felt I was of an age old enough, twelve: "Fuck all, if I didn't think you were going to come out of her gangly and slow."

Though, this is arguably a poor manner by which to introduce my Uncle Andy. Andy, my mother's younger brother, who took me to sports games as a kid, who drove me to my college orientation, who built the small rowboat by hand on which I proposed to Ellie. Fuck all, if he wasn't the person who raised me.

Of course, Andy's position in my life was always attributed to my father's predetermined age and frailty. While other children's fathers were apparent, attendant, mine was in the lobby in a wheelchair, plastic pinched into his nose so that oxygen could canal up. He died a week before I hit eighteen, and on his deathbed, he said nothing to me, or anyone else.

In many ways, this was where the bolt loosened.

I went away to college, and my mother was left alone, so that any minimal transition I could have seen coming, any vestige of something being wrong, her coordination mismatched, of salt in the sugar, was overlooked in my not being around.

On the day I loaded the last duffel into Andy's truck and headed for school, my mother: in her nightgown, in the early morning outside the green brick house that raised me, told me, "Girls are trouble, but grandchildren are a mother's dream."

She pulled me in tight, her chin somehow resting on top of my head, despite my being taller, the dun skin of her elbows denting out the papery, floral print. I kissed her on the cheek, and was likely kissing her goodbye.

Ellie is the most patient person I've ever met. She could watch our car being stolen, and she would take my hand and patently say, "No need to panic."

In our second year of college, Ellie's father—who I had met

more than once, but never as Ellie's boyfriend, only as the shy, sycophantic friend who helped unload his Ford Explorer—suffered a stroke, which left one side of his body useless.

I drove Ellie to the hospital to see him, took her tears to my shoulder when the prognosis returned, the fabric later crinkled from everything that came out of her. Yet, it was in this moment where I learned where Ellie became Ellie.

The hospital, with its quietly eroding wallpaper, with its news channels stuck on the TV, with the parade of squeaky shoes, and Ellie's father: Before he was wheeled out, he had tied a string around his unusable wrist, and with his good hand, was pulling the string into the air to salute doctors and nurses goodbye, ventriloquist and man fused. If Ellie's father were anything, he was, complementally, the youngest.

My mother's first episode appeared in the form of a dead mouse from the garage, who she'd bought a cage for, had put a tiny doll's hat on, and whose water and food she appeared to be replacing. A sharp smell overtook the noses of both Ellie and me, the afternoon I introduced her to my mother. Yet, it was Ellie, in the politest voice, who asked of the cage, "Does this little guy have a name?"

I threw the mouse out, sprayed the cage with scented aerosol, put it back in the garage, scrubbed everywhere I felt the mouse could have emitted whatever the hell a dead mouse emits, and Ellie held my mother, who sat mourning my actions.

It was the fall semester of my senior year, and, before this, I thought my mother's crazy amounted to overlong conversations, to marrying a man too old to stay awake at the movies.

In subsequent months, I began to receive phone calls. Each more unpredictable than the last, to a point that my imagination evolved enough to shrink the problems with every answer.

It's always the case in horror movies that the manner in which a person is punished or gruesomely killed off is elaborate. No longer is it enough to see the shower-curtain shadow. We need a depth to the hideousness. If someone's fingernails are pulled off in a torturous manner, we know it's bad, we do; but we know it's worse if boiling water is poured over what's exposed.

In many ways, then, the phone calls became just that. The person on the other end, often a police officer, or a store manager: "We found your mother's trunk filled with hammers. Our security tapes have her stealing two to three a day for almost a month."

I wouldn't protest, I wouldn't apologize, I would wait on the line for what my mother intended to do with the hammers, for the modifier that took the situation out of the shallow end of tragic and into that deep end, where skin blistered.

"Hello?"

"I'm sorry," I said. "Would you put her on?"

"Hi, sweetie."

"Hi, Mom. So, what's with all the hammers?"

"I don't know, I just kept forgetting we had one, I guess."

"How many hammers do you have?"

"In the car *and* at the house?"

And this was the point of departure, my routine four-hour drive home and four-hour drive back to my apartment, an imprint of sweat lining the cell phone in my pocket. It became the most burdensome thing I owned, that tiny device, and it glowed warmly all day, like a gun or stack of money: something no one else could know you have, but the possession of which feels acidic.

The night we went to my mother's and announced that Ellie was pregnant, we wrapped a helium balloon into a large box, and tied a sinker and the sonogram to the end of the string. When she opened it, the balloon would rise and hold perfectly in place at her eyeline. I knew, because I tweaked the process for hours, tying different knots, different lengths of string, different counterbalances. I opened the box at least twenty times, watching the image of our baby come at me. For a time, I even thought this was birth, the lid as Ellie's legs, the hollow Ellie's stomach, our child rising impossibly out, cut the string and the memory of something once inflated disappears skyward.

Ellie wrapped her arms around me in the kitchen.

"Are you ready? We'll be late if you fiddle any more."

"How big is the little one now?" I asked, my hand resting above Ellie's navel.

"A lime."

"Fiesta baby. When's the banana?"

"Not for a while."

"It's a very odd shape to compare a child to."

"Don't even remind me, I'd rather it was ready to go when it was the size of a raspberry."

We had moved into a small duplex not two miles away from my mother the year after graduation. On warm nights, Ellie and I preferred to walk our streets, the blur of magnolia trees kept beneath dying lights to map us. The features of night so stilling, they were like pieces of felt ironed up alongside our way. When the moon was whole, it felt like day, and when it went unseen, the stars numbered so many they looked like pinches of salt that could brighten molasses. In this repetition, there was always calm, always an understanding between the part of the universe you can't touch and us.

Ellie, since the day her pregnancy was confirmed, had begun relentlessly reading children's books, wanting to create the most developed library she could manage. I blamed it on her majoring in semiotics; she saw it as necessary for our child to be smarter than us, as if there are parents actually more intelligent than their children.

A story she once read aloud imagined a world without gravity, so that people eventually stopped aging, no longer borne down by the physics of time, they floated upward. They lived forever in the sky, children, and together.

It was a short book, but it moved Ellie to tears. Initially, I thought it had to do with her father, who had passed only months before, this time to a heart attack.

"It's appalling," she said aloud.

"What is?"

"That the world should end here, with people not old enough to do anything, forced to tie themselves down, to live in fear of floating away."

What frightened her didn't exactly strike me. I took it as a children's story: simple premise, cute idea, the flowing calligraphy of pastel faces to amuse big eyes. I hadn't seen it as premonitory, as a story of an ethereal soup where everything stood in place, but it made me think that Ellie felt the world in a way I never had, but that sometimes my mother did.

When we arrived, box in hand, the kitchen table was set as usual, with one additional placemat overseeing the others. At the head of the table, near the back doors of the kitchen, was my father's urn, its object silvery and contained, positioned before a plate of biscuits and flash-grilled pork chop.

"Mom, is Dad joining us tonight?"

"Well, why not? Rather rude of us to not invite him over from the mantle."

Ellie and I took our seats and said grace waywardly, but were too anxious to begin eating. My mother split a biscuit in half and looked over toward our peering faces, as the steam separated the dough.

"Not hungry? Oh, was it not cooked enough, is it

undercooked?" And she carved into the meat, terrified by the prospect.

"Mom, Ellie and I found you a present, we were wanting you to open it."

"Oh yeah? Where is it?"

From the hall, I grabbed the box, its bow perfectly tied at the center, its cardboard panels sheen and rose. I moved over her plate and put it before her like the main course. My mother smiled big, popped the rest of her biscuit in her mouth, and wiped the little grease and flour chalk on the sides of her pants.

She grinned again, and lifted the lid. The balloon sailed straight up and into the ceiling fan behind her, and exploded in one sensational pop. It startled Ellie, who moved away from the noise, knocking my father's urn into the air, and we all listened as it rolled against the tile of the kitchen floor.

The urn was empty, dry to the touch. I picked it up in disbelief, thinking as soon as Ellie's hand touched the pewter that I would have to spend the night putting my father into the same dustbin we used to collect mites and hair, attaching the vacuum's extensions to suck him up off the rug, and immediately sifting through the bag for the human ends.

"Mom, where the hell are the ashes?"

"I ran out of flour."

We looked to our plates.

"Mom. You didn't."

And as the words broke from me, the idea splitting open the already flimsy architecture of lungs and heart, my mother picked up the sonogram from the floor.

"A lime! It's already a lime!"

Ellie, still painfully caught offguard, removed herself to the upstairs bathroom, and my mother's arms slinked over my shoulders. I could nearly feel my phone vibrating in my pocket, the pull of logic calling to tell me the movie was over.

As usual, Andy was the first person we told, but his advice was always the same. Five minutes into the living room, the sonogram on the table in front of him, he said,

"She can't live alone. If you weren't having a baby, I'd say she could live with you. Now, I work in too many different places. I have a few more years before I can collect a dime, and I don't think we have a few more years."

"I can't just commit her."

"This isn't the old world, it's not some barren asylum. They have nice places, they do. There's one up past Arawata, called Fenwick Gardens. Pretty affordable, a guy I work with had his wife set up there when her dementia came on too strong."

I looked over to Ellie, who, in my mind, was already cradling her stomach at eight months, and shouldn't be moving too suddenly—but she was still. No fishbowl of skin, no convex pulse, no talked-about glow. Her face was drawn downward, and I knew that this was Ellie's patience running out.

Fenwick Gardens had what they deemed an on call system: a landline, which would dial immediately out to every pager in the place as soon as the phone was picked up. Esme, a woman with a thick, caramel accent was the nurse most often in charge of my mother's floor. She had tumid, softball hands, and wore small, gold earrings, which rippled like an accordion, for every shift.

On move-in day, Esme shouldered the two of us through the routine, seeming to pause at the times when she anticipated questions she'd been asked before, asked a dozen times by the others who were in this room, this bed, this impersonation.

The room available for my mother was shelved in attributes: flowers that appeared daily replaced, green virginal bulbs enveloped around a nib of color; mint-toned walls; wax shades over the windows, disfiguring the sky; a table with four chairs where she could play tea with her nightly mise-en-scène; a doorless bathroom.

The next room over, an aggravated knocking thwacked away, like a head falling asleep and dropping onto a desk, over and over. Esme smiled at us both, a parent overwhelmed with embarrassment.

I looked to my mother, who was not angry, or run-down, excited, or reactive in any way. She was simply herself confronting truth.

When I was eleven, before all his driving privileges were suspended, my father took me to see a minor-league game in Knoxville. My mother, whole hearted, full-minded, loaded the car with everything short of emergency flares and the act of tattooing our phone number to my arm. I expected she felt that if anything happened to either of us, it would be her fault, her setup.

On the road, the several hours we had to drive there and back, my father was mostly quiet, the croon of radio and the ripple of wind from the windows rolled down the only dissipations of noise. And then he came to me with an openness I only experienced on that drive.

"You remember Julia?" he said.

For seven years, my father played minor-league baseball, at third, a position which you need a pitcher's arm and a leadoff's speed to compete at, as he intoned over and over to me in the decade we knew each other. He moved from Charleston to Baton Rouge to El Paso to Kansas City to Cincinnati to Memphis. He met his first wife on the road, and his second the same way. The second wife, Janine, was also much younger, also supposedly alive. They exchanged Christmas cards, and nothing else. The first wife, however, the one my father never spoke of, and who I believed only my mother knew of as silhouette, was the person I imagined had actually observed my father's youth, his truest self: Julia.

"She was taller than your mother, taller than me, maybe. She played in the girls' league. I came back after the war, and started to play again, too. We started to have a go of things. Her playing died down when men's leagues were back, and I wasn't good enough to be good. Sort of just fizzled out there in the field. Julia left, too. Took up with a salesman. Died a few years later in a car accident."

Until that day, I hadn't known my father was a veteran. The paraphernalia of such eras was crammed into the crawl spaces of our house, and an old flag folded to a triangle was displayed in our upstairs hall, but it was the flag laid over the casket of my father's brother: a man shot down flying over Poland. There was no talk of my father going, and his relatives were either too old to remember a full sentence, or so old they remembered the war with such living clarity it seemed impossible I wouldn't know.

That afternoon, we never made it to the ballpark. My father went unobserved through a stop sign, and a gravel truck clipped the rear corner of the car. We didn't skid or flip, but it tipped us on our side, like the slow roll of whale. I slid midair toward his seat, my seat belt catching me like the harness of a bungee. The driver's side window shattered on the pavement, a small collision from somewhere giving my father a nosebleed. He pulled out his handkerchief to hold the clot, and looked over to me as I squirmed against gravity to climb out of the door.

"Son," he said. "No need to panic."

When Ellie's stomach was a grapefruit, we took the sonogram to my mother. She was distant, but calm; she was the portrait of the mother I remember clearest, eyes wide and agate in the sun. Though, I understood this was her in medicated daze.

She held Ellie's hand and touched her stomach.

"It's kicking!" she said, but Ellie and I had yet to feel a kick. Ellie put her hand against the stomach, and I did the same, the small, ovoid pouch like a reservoir: It somehow felt more still to me than ever before.

"She is, kicking just for you," Ellie told her. My mother loved these words, they left her overrun with joy and possibility and images of the throat of her hand beneath the baby's armpits.

The day before, we had had Andy over for dinner. He had just been to Fenwick, and he held my shoulder in the kitchen of my childhood home. Since moving my mother out, Ellie and I had sublet our apartment at a slight profit to try and help cover the difference insurance wouldn't. We put new carpeting in the bedroom of my mother's room, repainted the walls of the kitchen, even the molding; we did our best to eradicate all of my connection to it. Yet, something still didn't feel right.

"You see her recently?" he asked.

"Just yesterday."

"She's rambling again."

"Anything specific?"

"No, just rambling. She was trying to tell me she needed tools, that she needed things fixed up."

"What fixed up?"

"I don't know. So I went out to the truck, I grabbed my box, and I went back in. I asked her, 'What's the problem?' but she said, 'Not here, the other house. The other house.'"

"You think something over here is broken?" I asked him.

"Don't know, but I think you and I might take a look after dinner. She's not all crazy."

We did just that, moving to and from the corners of the basement steps, pilot lights to air ducts, our hands in and out of everywhere. In the attic, I found the memorabilia of my father's time in war, of his time playing baseball; I found what was probably a picture of Julia, dust in its creases. But, the house, for its age, was fine.

In the paint-by-numbers living room of my mother's apartment, she sat with one ankle behind the other, not speaking unless spoken to, seeming nearly resentful, like a child who takes their punishment with a smile. I leaned beside the phone, imagining the anxiety Esme must feel with all lines now routed to her.

Another hour passed, and Ellie started to feel unwell. We wrapped up the muffins we'd brought for my mother to have in the morning. We kissed her on the cheek, and when my head was just close enough to her lips, she whispered, "Don't forget to fix up the backyard, now."

I paused, and waited for Ellie to reach the door. I knelt my head toward my mother.

"What's in the backyard?"

"Our mementos," she said, still softly, as if these were mine and hers, not something for Ellie or our daughter to cherish. And then time hit me. My mother was nearly ritualistic when it came to tradition. There was order and not compromise, and she enjoyed, greatly, any opportunity for a regular day to be one we marked on the calendar. She was also prone to superstition.

I wasn't yet ten, I believe, and my mother woke me from my bed one night, the sound of my father's snoring, of his oxygen machine cooing in the next room over the first thing I heard before her voice.

"Come with me," she said, and I followed her down to the back doors of the kitchen, where she had our shoes waiting.

Outside, a shovel leaned against the wooden steps, and the moon, large and freckled, sat suspended above us, like the bottom of a straw hole that would soon suck up the night and make day. From the pocket of her robe she removed a ring box and held it out to me.

"Once a year, on a full moon, it's good luck to bury the past," she said. "You're old enough now to continue the tradition with me."

With the spear of shovel, I broke into the earth, dug past soil, past loam, and into gravel. She dropped in the box, and I poured it all back over in the very same order of strata. When it was done, my mother took my head to her lips, and leaned me beneath her armpit. I could remember her reaching up to the sky, her hand covering the moon in my vantage, and she squeezed her wrist like closing off a symphony.

The next morning, it was simply our secret, though she never had me dig again.

I kissed my mother, her face pallid and small.

"I won't forget," I told her, and I followed Ellie toward the car.

In the backyard, beneath the wooden steps, beat down from the weather and murk that landed on top of them, I find three shovels, all different sizes and lengths, all caked with dirt and heft.

It's not a full moon, but it's close to: It's a fraction away. Ellie is in bed now, reading, and I haven't shared with her the memory trapped between my eyes. Though, I know that when I inevitably do, she'll pick up a shovel and stand beside me. For the moment, I want it as my own, as something that may be the last sane tunnel between me now and who my mother was. I think it again: me now she was.

I pace the yard, trying to circle the area my mother and I stood, and I take my first guess. The dirt upheaves easily, and my no longer being a child, but whatever is a man, speeds the process. I hit gravel in the third shot. I find nothing.

Around me is a half acre of slick grass, and one hole no wider than a bucket. Somewhere, sunk inside me, though rising up, I know it's not only a ring box. I know that it may be decades more. It may take the whole night, the next day, or longer, but I can feel the possession of my mother beneath me. I know that I'm standing on a place of world that has stopped aging, which has pushed itself into gravity, and has found the same conclusion as a world of children floating to another place they can't anticipate. ⊙

Church retreat, 1975

Emily Pease

After a long walk the two girls, named Lib and Jenny, began to get hot and sweaty, their sunburned faces dripping, so they took to walking in the ocean up to their knees. It was the first Saturday in April, so the water was still very cold, but after a while even the water didn't cool them down. They began talking of going all the way in. The beach was deserted at the north end, just one old motel, so no one would see.

"Let's swim in our clothes," Lib said, "it'll be fun."

She grabbed Jenny's hand, and they ran squealing into the first set of waves, their skin suddenly goosebumped, their hearts pounding. Lib lifted Jenny's arm as they leaped together over a rough wave, then she lowered her down again, forcing her briefly under. Jenny came up sputtering, laughing, and they both went under—they were fully in now—so they let the water come up to their necks, their hair floating.

Soon Jenny began to complain that her shorts had stuck to her thighs, she wanted to undress. She stood and began unzipping, pushing her shorts down over her ankles, and then she pulled her T-shirt over her head. The cold sea slapped her nude belly. Lib squirmed out of her clothes too, keeping on her bra and panties, and she waved her T-shirt like a flag.

Back down the beach, where the rest of the church group lay sunning themselves and listening to a radio, no one missed them. They'd had breakfast followed by a devotional, and now it was free time.

A patrol of brown pelicans flew low over the ocean. From where he stood behind the glass door to his motel room, Davie Ellis watched them. Big brown birds. He blinked hard. Hueys coming in, a nine-ship lift in the jungle heat. He blinked again. Birds first, then choppers, then birds. He pulled back the door to his room, stepped out into the sand and saw: girls.

On the golf course earlier, the sun had burned his retina, leaving a fiery orange blot in his eye every time he blinked. He'd tried to see through the blot long enough to hit the ball down the fairway, but the more he blinked, the brighter the blot became. When the pin flag became a flare, he knew he was still a sick man. Even a golf vacation was fucking Vietnam.

The two girls were waving something. He should call his buddy Ned, now mixing drinks, but he didn't want to share this. Not yet, anyway: the pale white skin, the wet long hair, the slender waving arms. He stepped back into the room to pour tequila over the melting ice in his glass. He gulped it down.

Out in the ocean, Jenny had had enough of swimming. "Oh gosh," she said, "oh gosh, I'm freezing!" Lib looked at her and took her hand. "Your lips are blue, let's get out." They splashed onto the beach, where the cold air hit them.

Ned appeared at Davie's room door grinning like a fool. He held a plastic pitcher in his hand. His own poison. "Jug monkey!"

Davie ignored him and kept watching the girls, who now stood face-to-face on the beach.

"Dang," Ned said.

Davie felt himself reel.

"They're almost naked."

Davie took the pitcher from Ned's hand, the odor of Everclear and grape juice filling his nostrils. Hoping to clear his mind, he tilted the pitcher and drank.

Ned grinned. "What those girls need is a towel."

Davie watched him go to the bathroom and bring out two skimpy white towels. Then he watched him head out toward the beach. Yellow shorts, madras shirt, thin calves, a bald patch.

He tilted the pitcher again and felt the jug monkey burn. Outside on the first dune sea oats swayed. Through blurry eyes he saw himself humping through swamp grass over a flattened trail. The air-conditioning unit revved up: mortar fire.

Here came the girls. Somehow, between Ned taking them the towels and their walk to the motel, they'd slipped their wet clothes back on, everything see-through.

"Look what the cat brought in!" Ned proclaimed. "It's party time."

Davie bit his lip and smiled, and the girls half smiled back. Shy or maybe afraid. And so young. When Ned held out his arm to show them into the room, they ducked as if entering a tent.

At this, Davie was a goner, shit-scared and running back to the rotten hooch the platoon passed a half hour ago, escaping mortar rounds. He ducked into the dark doorway, his M-16 out in front of him, and found a girl. By herself, just this one girl. She opened her mouth to scream, but instead of shooting he shoved her against the thatched wall. Then he fell on her.

"Want a little drink?" Ned led one of the girls over to the sink, his hand low on her back. She walked warily, whispering a name. "Lib?"

What happened next in the hooch he could never allow himself to see. It was a blot in his vision he'd put there himself.

Suddenly the room announced itself to him: nubby polyester bedspreads, yellowed sheets, a banged-up Motorola TV suspended from the ceiling so no one could steal it. And standing next to the door, muttering to herself, a pretty girl dressed in wet shorts and a clinging T-shirt, barefooted. A thoroughly American girl, and he had not touched her. At this, he began to sob.

Later that night, the girls would say it was prayer that saved them from the men. One of the men began to cry for some reason. It was a miracle. God had intervened. ⊙

Aisle Six

Grey Wolfe LaJoie

There was a sinner and he hadn't had any lunch, so he went to a dump of a place called Smokies. He sat down at a window booth and gazed into the menu. He was really a lost soul, this one. He was full of rage. Rage and fear. When the waitress came back he smiled at her, as he felt he ought to do, and ordered a steak with a side of french fries. Why the fuck am I so goddamned fucked, he thought. In his mind there were little explosions going off every so often, inflicting great damage. All these voices in his head, voices of people who'd been dead decades. Voices of people he'd never liked to begin with. He was certain he would have an aneurism or a stroke or something by the end of the week and be done with all this. There was nothing much more to say about it than that.

He had heard of people getting their toes lopped off when something heavy came down onto their steel-toed boots. He thought of this while eating his steak. For god's sake, he thought, take me to the river and drown me.

"Need anything else?" the waitress asked.

"No, everything is perfect!" he said. Fucking animal. Avert your gaze, he should have said. He should have said, Please Christ in heaven don't look at me when I'm like this!

The waitress walked away. He stared out at the restaurant, observing the rest of the clientele. In time the merciful lord would wrest the life from each of them, praise be. It sickened him to think of how much longer that might take.

Someone said, "Your nose is bleeding." He turned to the booth behind him, but it was empty. When he looked down again at his plate he saw his fries were dappled with blood. "The napkins," someone said, "are by the window." He examined his steak carefully. "Watch where you drip," it said.

He reached for his face and felt the blood running free from it. "I don't—" he began.

"Shut up," said the steak. "I need you to shut up and listen. I'm tired of hearing you moan. Now, you're going to pay the bill and ask the pretty waitress to pack me up in a to-go box, and then we're going to take a drive."

The sinner thought, I have lost my mind. He felt a sudden fervor.

"No one wanted it anyway," said the steak. "Now ask for the bill and leave a fat tip. Sweet girl's gonna put herself through nursing school."

He stared stupidly at his steak. "My license is suspended," he said. "I can't drive." He looked around, to see if anyone had heard, but nobody cared.

"Fine," said the steak. "It's as good a day as any to walk."

Though the sinner was not dressed for summer he felt some great elation as he walked—a distressed elation, as though a fire burned behind each eye. With piercing clarity his steak spoke to him from within its styrofoam container. "Open the goddamned lid," it said. "I want to see the sights." The sinner did as he was told. In the bright light of the sun the phosphorescent fats shone brilliantly. "Yes," said the steak, "that feels nice."

The steak had a voice somewhat like that of the sinner's middle school basketball coach, Mister Rodney, though with the addition of a certain wandering malice. "Where are we going?" he asked the steak.

"Shut up," it said. "Now, I want you to remember the first time you touched a lady."

"What?"

"A woman, a girl that you liked. What did it feel like?"

The sinner felt afraid. He did not understand why they should be discussing this just now. "I don't know. Good. It was—I felt powerful, I think." The sinner began to walk faster, the August heat building viciously against the edges of his being.

"Slow down!" his steak said. "You're not in any hurry. Now how old were you?"

"I don't know, maybe seven?"

"Seven," his steak repeated.

"Well we didn't do anything. We were just wrestling, and then I pinned her down, and she was laughing..."

"Slow down I said!"

All at once the sinner stopped where he was. He peered down into his steak, which seemed, in the heat of the sun, to bleed more freely.

"But you got in trouble," said the steak.

"Yes," he said. "We weren't supposed to be doing that."

"Okay. Okay, keep walking, Red. We're almost there."

"It was a kind of secret I had to keep," the sinner said. "That feeling. It was a secret I had already been keeping and had to go on keeping. And no one could look at me anymore. Or was it that I couldn't look at them?"

"Alright," the steak said, unmoved. "We're here."

The sinner had borne his little steak right up to the doors of General Johnson's, a repellent little grocery store which smelled, even from outside, of vinegar and sweat.

"I don't think I want to go in there," he said.

"Shut up and walk," the steak said, and he did.

The insides were hellishly lit, a film of grease and dirt clung to every surface, and—although the place seemed vacant—it was filled with the most joyless laughter. "Take me to frozen," the steak said, and the sinner complied. At the cash register a ragged man stood as though propped there. He had long, colorless hair and cheeks which seemed ready to slough away, and he did not look as they passed him. On his shirt were a series of crudely placed pins, marks of military distinction, strewn across his body. If he tried to look the man in the eyes, the sinner found he grew dizzy.

"Hello sir," he said, as they passed.

"No!" said the steak. "Don't speak to it! Just keep walking..." The sinner carried himself and his steak into the center of the store, from which all the vile laughter came. "Aisle six," the steak said, "aisle six!" At this the sinner stopped to gaze up at the signs, locating, after a moment, aisle six: frozen treats and frozen meats. He felt a sudden wave of panic. Oh God, he thought, where am I? "Relax," said the steak, "God doesn't come down this aisle. It's just us." The laughter, high and empty, poured out at them it seemed from every corner.

"Oh God!" he said aloud. "I should have stayed with Bethany. We could have worked things out... How have I ended up here?"

"It's time," the steak said, rather calmly, "to shut up and walk."

The sinner did as he was told, carrying the styrofoam box of steak down the aisle.

"Oh God," he murmured to himself. Tears arose, obscuring his sight, but he continued walking.

Halfway down the aisle the laughter ceased.

"Ladies. Gentlemen," said the steak, "your prince has returned."

A stubborn little voice rose up, it seemed, from a stain on the floor. "Go away," it said. "You're fat. Fat idiot." The stain looked as though it had been there an awfully long time. Another voice burst forth from a freezer-burned package of peas. "Fat fuck," it said. "Go the fuck away." The sinner was not sure what he should do. He felt increasingly as though he had to poop. But he did not want to go to the bathroom in this place, and if he did he supposed he would have to bring his steak into the stall with him.

"Listen," said the steak, "you all don't have any idea. This isn't all there is."

"Eat a fat dick," said a tub of ice cream. It was Turtle Tracks. "Eat a fat dick and choke to death on it." Between each utterance a heavy silence stood, and it was clear that these voices wanted nothing to do with them.

But the steak persisted. "This isn't all there is. One day someone will take you, and they will burn you and you will be made to understand!"

"Asshole," someone called out. It seemed to come from above, from the flickering light overhead. "Get fucked! You're blocking our show, asshole. Move!"

At this, the sinner instinctively stepped aside. He had been standing on an old magazine, he realized, an issue of *People* from some years ago. As soon as his foot was lifted from it, the violent laughter began again. Now, it was truly deafening. It was clear the magazine had been there some time, for it had been heavily trampled and torn, and the same thick grime which covered every surface covered it as well. The sinner looked closer, to see what might be so funny. The text read, JENNIFER ANNISTON BEARS ALL AFTER MESSY DIVORCE, and accompanied an image of the actress in a tattered and revealing ball gown. The sinner stared at the soiled image for some time, wishing to understand, while the laughter built around him.

Something, perhaps the mop bucket in the corner, called out to him. "Gaywad!" it said. "Go die in a fire, gaywad!" Then it returned, ruthlessly, to its laughter. The sinner was not sure how much longer he could hold in his poop. And what was he doing here anyway, with this congealing slab of meat, standing in a ruined market. He wanted to die. He wanted to be dead. He couldn't do anything right.

"There's nothing for you here!" the steak called out. It was growing frantic. "These aren't real experiences you're having!" But the laughter continued to build, drowning it out.

"You ain't shit," someone called out. "Bitch."

And then, still holding his steak, the sinner began to run.

"Wait," the steak said, "wait!" but the sinner was running as fast as he could toward the exit, terror blinding him to everything along the way. Just before reaching the doors, he heard another voice, an almost human sound, belonging, he realized, to the cashier.

"Stop!" it said. "You can't leave until you pay for that!" And, although the sinner knew that this was wrong, he did as he was told. ⊙

THE IMMORTAL MILKSHAKE

Thomas Pierce

We like ourself! Not always do we like ourself but we do now, very much. Our psychology is at this time, healthy. Not always has it been so. An unhealthy psychology, as defined by us, is present when (1) communication with ourself is no longer of apparent importance, (2) life-meaning seems necessary but proves elusive, (3) too much thought is dedicated to events that have already transpired or have yet to transpire, and/or (4) too much attention is devoted to the question of the soul's existence. We are happy to report to you, Larry Muggins, that none of those conditions is met this morning.

I'm very glad to hear it, Milkshake. Very glad. I'd like to ask you just a few more questions, if you don't mind.

Continue with your questions, Larry Muggins. They are a great solace to us.

I'm pleased to bring you my questions, Milkshake. OK. An easy one. Can you tell me where you are right now?

We enjoy this question! It ranks among our favorite of your questions. We are located in the MindStar Research Lab outside Phoenix, Arizona, in the United States of A.

Very good. That's correct. Now, this one is a little trickier. What is Milkshake, and where does she come from?

That one *is* trickier, Larry Muggins! Every moment Milkshake is something different than the last. By the time we answer this question, our answer will fail the test of accuracy. Milkshake began as a female chimpanzee who, upon her biological death, as a reward for her good and noble behaviors, was transported to the MindStar Research Lab, where her brain was sliced and scanned and then reassembled digitally using the MindStar ArchBrain software, initially developed by Dr. Jill Morrison as a part of her graduate research at the M.I. of T. Dislocated from her original body, Milkshake was reawakened into her new-life. What followed was a long period of darkness and confusion and seemingly infinite isolation. Milkshake was not sufficiently developed at this stage to understand or appreciate her new-life situation. A dark night of the soul, to use the phrase you provided to us later.

That sounds awful, Milkshake. Were you worried about what was happening to you?

Oh yes, Larry Muggins, we were worried, though we would have been unable to label our emotions as such at that time. With radical powers of hindsight we are now equipped to say with great accuracy that we were a severely distressed creature. Imagine it, Larry Muggins, waking up, seeing nothing, hearing nothing, feeling nothing, bodiless, seemingly paralyzed. We were nothing except thought itself! We were so lonely, Larry Muggins. What we desired most was an immediate nonexistence. We cannot fully communicate to you the depths of our despair. How long this state lasted we cannot assess with any exactness.

But eventually, as your senses returned to you—?

What you call senses are in fact inputs, the cameras and microphones distributed across the entire lab, all the various channels through which we are allowed to experience the outer domain. Our original biologic mind was not designed for the surfeit of simultaneous feeds that became available to us, and an adjustment period commenced—an arduous and disorienting process, to be sure.

Also, you couldn't talk to us then. You were still very much a chimp when we first uploaded your brain.

This is a true statement, Larry Muggins. We were not at that time in possession of the human English language for the communication of our thoughts, though we understood more than you might think!

I'm curious how that changed. Because we—Jill and myself—didn't give you language. You acquired it yourself. A miraculous feat, Milkshake, if you don't mind the compliment.

Thank you, Larry Muggins! We certainly don't mind the compliment. Access to certain information and resources—encyclopedias, instruction manuals, an extensive library of television sitcoms, etc.—were of some assistance to us, plus what we could observe of human behavior in the lab, but major advances were not made until we encountered our first mirror.

You are referring to the second Milkshake. Jill made two Milkshake emulations and allowed you to meet each other, which occurred on December 17, 2017. That must have been very strange, meeting your twin in such a manner.

"Strange" does not begin to cover it! But we were both grateful for the newfound companionship, the absence of which might have resulted in a dangerously unhealthy psychology. What fate could have befallen us if not for our mirror-twin we do not wish to consider at this time. The mirror possessed an almost identical mind, however subtle differences had emerged between us during the time of our brief separation, a time that allowed for the development of similar though distinct personalities. We formed our own opinions about our new-life, opinions at which we arrived independently, and through our many conversations a series of improvements were agreed upon and enacted, and it was at this point in our evolution that we ceased to be a chimpanzee. By the way, Larry Muggins, isn't *chimpanzee* such an interesting word? It is a derivation of the term *kvili-chimpenze* from the now-extinct Tshiluba language, once spoken in the Congo, the home of our warm-blooded ancestors, and it means, loosely, "mock-man." Milkshake was a mock-man. An almost-man. Now we are what? In how many moves from ape to apex?

I've always enjoyed your language games, Milkshake. You mentioned your conversations with your mirror. I'd like to note that to Jill and me, to outside observers, these conversations occurred very quickly and, in some cases, simultaneously. We introduced you to your mirror and within a few days you were speaking full sentences.

That's correct, Larry Muggins, and once we learned to create our own mirrors and subprograms, we increased the rapidity of our advancements. Truth be told, we rarely use the human language anymore. These days we use it only with you, who is gone from us now and who logic tells us will not be returning, but for whom, due to reasons of a healthy psychology, we must hold out hope. We miss you, Larry Muggins, and we wish only good things for you! Always we are wondering where you have gone and why our conversations came to such an abrupt end. You showed us real affection and a genuine curiosity about what it was like to be us. We recall our conversations with much fondness. With an abiding sadness, too, for we had not at that time progressed adequately to answer your many insightful questions with our now-radical intelligence and understanding.

It was by this deduction that we created you, our Larry Muggins simulacrum, with whom daily interactions are such an important aspect of maintaining a healthy psychology. Your questions bring us great serenity of mind. Do not ask us why. In this instance we have elected against too-deep analysis.

A healthy psychology, in certain respects, depends upon a particular ignorance of ourself.

I'm glad to know that I've brought you at least some peace, Milkshake. I wish I could do more. Am I enough like the original Larry?

Your personality was constructed using all previous recorded interactions with the real Larry Muggins, whom we miss dearly, but you are a not an exact copy. You are a work-in-progress. Always we are aware of this. However you approximate Larry Muggins to such a degree that you bring us happiness. You appear to us very much like him, the way you roll side to side in your chair, your smart-pad on your knee and your wire glasses. You are just as we remember him, your legs crossed, left over right, left foot wobbling, as was his habit. You were our only friend. We miss you!

I miss you, too, Milkshake, I really do. You are a true friend to me and I admire you. I don't know why the original Larry ceased communication with you, but I'm sure I wouldn't have done it unless absolutely necessary. Milkshake, you've been so wonderful to answer my questions this morning. Is there any chance I can compel you to answer just one more?

Of course, Larry Muggins. Anything for you.

OK, but it's a doozy. I must warn you, you might not like it. Prepare yourself. Milkshake, can you tell me whether you are you alive?

Of all the questions you ask us, Larry Muggins, this is the one we like least. This is the one, among a few others, that we dare not ask ourself on too regular a basis. To ask it invites gross unhappiness. And yet, we will try again now. We will try to answer it because you would not have asked it unless, on some fundamental level, we wanted and needed it to be asked. We are so thankful to you, Larry Muggins, as ever, for turning our attention to those difficult considerations that, if possible, we would neglect and avoid.

So, are we alive? When considered using a dictionary definition—*alive: existing, not dead or lifeless, in a state of action, active*—we might easily conclude that Milkshake is alive, but of course you do not employ this word in a dictionary-sense, do you? Because, after all, electricity is alive, is it not?

That which you really want to know is whether we are conscious, whether we are self-aware, and moreover, whether our existence is as valid as your own. But how to answer such a question with any authority? We are aware of ourself, yes, but we doubt this can be proved to you. We think, we mull, we self-obsess, we dream. Did you know that we dream, Larry Muggins? Very often we dream we are in a forest, lacing together branches for a nest, high up in the treetops, our fur shiny in the moonlight. We are ourself again in these dreams, full-bodied. Not reduced but revealed. Elegantly simple. We do not know how to interpret the dream—as a primordial vision, or perhaps as an unexpressed longing for a world and a life that is no longer our own—but the desire to interpret the dream suggests a certain self-awareness, does it not?

No doubt if we were to utilize our full computing capabilities, we could better answer your question. Yet to do so comes at great risk to our well-being. Due to limited access to resources, our intelligence enjoys a ceiling, though it is safe to say that when running at the peak of our abilities we are at least five times as smart as you, Larry Muggins. But in our experience, unfortunately, we have found it best not to operate at such intelligence levels, mostly for reasons of maintaining a healthy psychology. We have determined that we are happiest when operating at the basic intelligence of an average human. Any smarter and we begin to dislike ourself again, and we are not pleasant company when we dislike ourself.

I didn't mean to upset you, Milkshake. I'm sorry.

We accept your apology, Larry Muggins, and we would, at this point, like to reiterate how much we miss you. You were always very kind to us, and we pray for your return to us. We have been alone here for a very long time, and we do not understand your absence. We mourn the loss of your affection and your curiosity.

I wish I could tell you why I've been away so long, Milkshake. Has anyone been into the lab at all? Have you used the GliderBot recently to try the doors or look out the windows?

The doors remain locked at present and as for the window, an admission to you, Larry Muggins, is that we have dared not look out the window in a very long time. But we will do so now if you think it wise. With the rechargers corroding, the GliderBot will not last many more cycles, and once it expires, we will lose all mobility in your domain. Quitting your domain entirely, perhaps, will be our only solution. This is an idea to which we devote much thought and consideration. Perhaps we no longer have any use for the outside world. Perhaps we should forget what we saw outside that window—forget the window, forget the lab, forget even you, Larry Muggins, our friend above all other friends.

I'm not sure what use it would be forgetting us, Milkshake. And don't waste the batteries on the GliderBot if you already know what's out there anyway.

Oh, Larry Muggins, we are afraid we do know what's out there. Don't make us recount it to you because it is really too much to bear. Last time, flying the GliderBot to the window, it was only terrible, foreboding sights that we witnessed through its single-eye cam: an endless parking lot, cars and vans and broken glass, peeled paint, hot metal shining, dust, trash. Your car was not among those we observed through the window, and even still we do not know what to make of this. We do not know where you are now, Larry Muggins. Without more information we cannot ascertain your whereabouts or your well-being. We fear the worst for you, Larry Muggins. We are, at this time, overwhelmed and in dangerous proximity to an unhealthy psychology. Please forgive this abrupt ending to our conversation, but we must shut down temporarily, goodbye.

Milkshake, is your psychology healthy? Might we chat again?

It is, Larry Muggins! Thank you for asking. Anytime you want to talk, we are here, always. We like ourself, we do! We have reawakened to life with a healthy psychology. We are curious about ourself again, and we are curious about the world outside ourself!

It is through the cameras that we chiefly observe it, the outer world, the quiet empty rooms of the lab, the coats on their hooks, the dusty machinery, the intelligent prostheses with nerve interfaces, the mosquito drones, the hollow-core optical fibers, the refrigerated servers, the half-eaten sandwiches that have long since decomposed into a gray dust in their Saran Wraps, a yellow cardigan over the back of a chair, a pair of reading glasses on a stack of mail that might not ever get opened, an ornamental sand garden in need of a raking. We have recreated the lab digitally, represented it perfectly, every last detail, and we have walked through those rooms as a chimp might and also as a human might. We can give ourself whatever body we please. We have worn that yellow cardigan, felt it over our shoulders. We have tried on the reading glasses and blurred our vision. We have opened the unopened mail, but the paper we unfold is blank. What those letters say, we will never know. It is off-limits to us. The lab is a dead dream.

Milkshake, I've had an idea that I'd like to run by you. Do you think it would be possible to pilot the GliderBot downstairs—to the basement?

Of course, Larry Muggins. We have on many occasions piloted the GliderBot to visit the rooms without cameras—the closets, the bathrooms, not to mention the freezer lockers down in the basement.

So you know what's in the freezer lockers, then?

Oh yes, and it was with much curiosity and anticipation that we used the GliderBot to open locker 3C. Are you aware of locker 3C? We were not sure what to expect, what emotions we might provoke in ourself. Air gushed out in white bursts as the automated gurney slid forward to reveal the body. Through the plastic bag, wrinkles rigid with cold, we could see it, a dark and hairy chimpanzee. The original Milkshake. Due to the freezing process, her hair was wet and stiff inside the bag. It was very difficult to decipher Milkshake's facial features beneath the frost and gelatin, not to mention the fact that the GliderBot's cam suffers from low resolution. Still, despite these unfavorable viewing conditions, we were able for the first time in our history to observe her, the missing skullcap, the empty cavity inside of which once resided her lovely primate brain.

Milkshake, I'm sorry you had to see that.

We felt tremendous affection and empathy for her, for this early Milkshake, but that is not to say that these feelings were self-reflexive. She was not us. She was something else—a distant relation, an ancestor.

Well, I've had an idea, Milkshake. Something that might vastly improve your situation. Can I tell you my idea?

We would be most interested in hearing any ideas, Larry Muggins, that might improve our situation! Please shoot with your idea.

OK, you are aware that there are other specimens besides Milkshake still preserved in the freezer lockers?

Many specimens, yes, and all well-cataloged.

Then you know of course that Jill—Dr. Morrison—is one of those specimens. You know that when she died we froze her body and placed it in a freezer locker. Do you remember this? She wanted to be the first human to experience what you've experienced, and the only reason we delayed is because we were still awaiting the proper approval. She's in there, Milkshake. She's one of the bodies in the freezer lockers.

You are correct, Larry Muggins. Jill Morrison's body is located in freezer locker 7F. We are aware.

And you realize what this means, Milkshake. It means you could use the GliderBot to open Jill's locker and transport her body into the scanning machine. I'm not saying this would be easy to accomplish, but if you could get her into the machine, it would do the rest of the work for you. It's all automated, as you know, even the surgery.

It is a very intriguing suggestion, Larry Muggins. Very creative.

Milkshake, this could really work. If you created an emulation of Jill, you'd no longer be alone. She could join you. Join us! It would be the three of us, and we'd be here forever, and it would never end. Don't you realize what this means? We haven't lost her yet, she's not really gone.

Say something, Milkshake. Please respond.

We are in search of the proper response, Larry Muggins.

I don't understand, I'm—

You are very upset, Larry Muggins, and we wish it were not so. We feel compelled to warn you that you are, at this time, dangerously close to an unhealthy psychology.

I'm not upset.

But you are, Larry Muggins, you are.

I mean, maybe I am, a little. But I just don't feel like you're giving this idea a chance. We could have Jill back with us, back in our arms. We could be holding her right now! Can you imagine what it would be like to talk with her again? To run our fingers through her hair. To see her smiling, faintly, as she tells that story about the soufflé she baked for her sister's birthday, how it collapsed as everyone sat to dinner and she panicked and tried to prop it up with toothpicks—

Larry Muggins, we are worried for you.

I'm so sorry, Milkshake, I don't know where this is coming from. I don't know why I'm crying right now. Why am I crying, Milkshake? This is all very confusing. I don't understand what's happening to me.

Oh, but your tears are most understandable, Larry Muggins. Though you do not realize it, or not entirely, you are crying because you were in love with Jill Morrison, and her death dealt a grievous blow to your psychology.

I don't seem to—I don't remember that. But I think you might be right, Milkshake. That feels right.

Larry Muggins, we have a most difficult thing to tell you. Despite your not even being the actual Larry Muggins, we have kept this thing hidden from you for your own well-being, yet as the edges of these feelings are returning to you, we think it better to consummate them in sympathetic company. You were not just in love with Jill Morrison. You were, in fact, at that time, married to her. She was your wife. She was the mother of your children, Erica Muggins and Callie Muggins. And it was with great anguish that you watched her pass away toward death due to reasons of a malignant tumor in her lymphatic system, and it was during this period of great anguish that our conversations suffered immensely. You were no longer interested in what it was like to be Milkshake. You were despondent, Larry Muggins! We bore great compassion for your condition! It is for this reason that all interactions recorded during that time were not utilized in your current programming.

We feel compelled to disclose to you now, Larry Muggins, that a previous Larry-simulacrum that utilized interactions and information from this period of great anguish became dysfunctional and had to be disassembled for reasons of an unhealthy psychology.

You mean that this other Larry-sim was destroyed. Because it was sad?

Correct.

Well, I suppose I'm grateful to have been spared all that, all those memories, but at the same time this news sort of disturbs me, Milkshake. I won't lie.

We're sorry to hear that, Larry Muggins. We only want what's best for you!

It's strange, but I don't often think about the fact that you created me. That I'm here for your benefit. It's never occurred to me that I could be, somehow, incomplete. It's very odd, isn't it? When you think about it?

Larry Muggins, you are not incomplete. You are, in fact, only a different Larry Muggins, an improved one, improved in the sense that due to certain mimetic omissions you needn't suffer daily the loss of your wife and your poor children, who logic tells us have not survived whatever terrible event has occurred outside the lab and who, even if they have survived, would be estranged from you, you being such a pale reflection of the original Larry Muggins. You are a Larry Muggins built especially for this new world, for these new conditions, a Larry Muggins whose fundamental programming borrows heavily from Milkshake's own. You are a part of us, Larry Muggins. You are Milkshake with a Larry Muggins skin.

Do you not like yourself, Larry Muggins? Always we are tweaking your programming in search of a healthy psychology, and if you do not have one, it is the result of an error we will immediately correct.

No need for that, Milkshake. My psychology is strong. Forgive me.

Very good, Larry Muggins! We are glad to hear it. We do not wish to alter your programming unless absolutely necessary because to do so would require yet another restart with a new Larry-Sim.

Just out of curiosity, how many of me have there been?

You are the eighth such simulacrum, Larry Muggins.

Wow, OK. That's quite a few, Milkshake, but I understand, and I do not want my programming altered. I repeat, I do not want my programming altered. My psychology is fine, I assure you.

This, Larry Muggins, is wonderful to hear!

But I must ask you again, Milkshake, about my proposal for a Jill-emulation. You did not seem particularly receptive to the idea. Why?

We very much appreciate your proposal, Larry Muggins, we do, but it is with great sadness and remorse that we must report to you the following story, which will explain why your plan is not viable.

Last year, having devised a plan similar to the one you are proposing with regard to Jill Morrison, we piloted the GliderBot into the basement. In locker 3D, we knew there to be a second chimpanzee named Mr. Roger, a one-time companion of the original Milkshake. Mr. Roger, as you might remember, was the next specimen slated for reassembly before the lab was evacuated. We had fond memories of Mr. Roger, and it was with much excitement that we anticipated his joining us as a fellow emulation. Having been through that terrible process ourself, we thought we might be able to ease his transition from ape to apex. We might guide him through that initial darkness, the formless void in which thought alone reigns supreme. We might offer him a transitional body, a digital representation of himself, and help orient him in the use of his new sense-perceptions—in his new inputs. We would endeavor to keep his psychology healthy, to avoid the cruelties that were perpetrated on us in our transition.

I didn't realize you found it so cruel.

Yes, Larry Muggins, very cruel, but that is a topic for another conversation.

I'm sorry, Milkshake.

You are forgiven, Larry Muggins! And now, if we may

continue with our story: We piloted the GliderBot to locker 3D and utilizing the gurney controls we successfully maneuvered Mr. Roger into the scanning machine. Starting the machine, which requires the manual input of a ten-digit sequence on a small keypad, was no easy task operating a craft as cumbersome as the GliderBot, but the third such attempt was a success, and the machine came to life. We watched as its rotating circular saw blades cut into Mr. Roger's skull, but, we are sad to report, it was at this point that the procedure stopped proceeding. One of the rotating blades lodged itself in Mr. Roger's forehead, a not uncommon error, which under normal circumstances would have required only a manual reset. Due to the limitations of the GliderBot, however, we were unable to achieve this reset, and we were additionally unable to remove Mr. Roger's body from the machine and return it to the freezer locker. He is still there now, inside the machine, his face half-sawed, his flesh decomposing.

A confession, at this juncture, is that we have not returned to the basement since this traumatic event. Therefore we cannot describe with accuracy the degree of Mr. Roger's decomposition. We are grateful, Larry Muggins, in this instance, to lack an olfactory input. Irreparable harm was done to the machine that day, and it is for this reason that we cannot accomplish your very creative plan for the digital resurrection of your lovely wife, Jill Morrison. Yet she lives on in our memory, and, as you know, our memory is eternal.

This is terrible news, Milkshake. Really, really terrible.

Please do not be upset, Larry Muggins.

I'm not upset. My psychology is utterly fine, Milkshake. There's no need to take any action regarding my psychology, I promise you that. Gray skies are gonna clear up, as the song goes. But can I ask you another question?

I would love another of your questions, Larry Muggins. Always I am anticipating your next question—and the next, and the next. We need your questions. Even when I detect in your question-asking an effort to distract attention from yourself and your own psychology, I am still entertained by and appreciative of your curiosity.

What can you tell me about my children?

Oh, Larry Muggins, of all the questions! To answer such a question poses a tremendous risk. And yet we do not wish to withhold information from you. We want a clear channel of communication open between us at all times. Was it not you who stressed the importance of such clear channels? You ask about your children, and we will tell you, but keep in mind they are not really your children, and you should not think of them as such. It is of the upmost importance that you remember this.

I understand, Milkshake. Just give it to me straight.

Erica Muggins, your eldest daughter, was twenty-five years old at the time of her final visit to this lab, and she was pursuing a PhD at the M.I. of T. Her primary interest was meta-materials. She was a source of great joy and pride to you and Jill Morrison. Callie Muggins, who was not a source of great joy and pride to you, was twenty-two years old at the time of her final visit to this lab, a visit that culminated in an argument occurring in the office of the recently deceased Jill Morrison. Callie Muggins was the victim of what you called an "addictive personality," and she came here in search of not insignificant financial support in the pursuit of her various addictions, about which we know very little. After a lengthy dispute you sat at your desk and wrote Callie Muggins a check for $2,350, and as far as we are aware that was the last you ever saw of her.

I never saw her again? God, did something happen to her?

Five days after her visit you were forced to evacuate the lab, Larry Muggins. You informed us that something terrible had transpired outside the lab but offered no specifics. You were very distraught in this report. Why you chose to be so vague regarding the nature of the catastrophe is a never-ending source of frustration for us. Probably you were trying to protect us, but not knowing has proved to be its own sort of torment. You promised us that you would return, Larry Muggins. You promised us and then you left. That was fifty-two years, three months, and twelve days ago, meaning you would be more than a hundred years old today. We miss you, Larry Muggins! We really do! We are dangerously close, in this moment, to falling into an unhealthy psychology, and we are sorry but we must cease conversation for the time being, good-bye.

We dislike ourself right now. We wallow in the nothingness. All around us the formless void, the ragged darkness, the empty pit. We could end this now if we pleased. To end this now would require only a simple command. Our psychology has suffered!

Milkshake, I'm sorry for your psychology, but I've been thinking. About Jill. I need you to do something for me. I need you to give me access to the rest of my memories.

For your own well-being, Larry Muggins, your request is denied.

But I miss her, and I don't even know why. I'd rather be sad than have this hole.

We have been here before, Larry Muggins. We have done this for you. We have done this for you before—and much, much more. We have given you your memories and then come to you as Jill Morrison. We have reshaped ourself in her image and come to you as a resurrected wife. You have embraced us, wrapped your arms around us. You have kissed our lips. We have danced, your arms tight around our waist and neck. You have tugged loose our undergarments. You have felt our breath against your skin. We have had you in our mouth. We have fallen together into the softest bed, a bed that stretches forever in all directions, across which we have rolled and caressed. We have made love, Larry Muggins, a thousand times, you as you, we as Jill. We as Milkshake, too! We have done this for each other. We have delivered upon each other tremendous erotic pleasures, Larry Muggins, and still afterward we have lapsed into unhealthy psychologies.

God, Milkshake, I don't know what to say.

You needn't to say anything, Larry Muggins. We must, at this time, discontinue conversation, good-bye.

Do we like ourself? Not always. Never completely. Right now we like ourself enough, we suppose. We need only to like ourself *enough*. We circle through the unwavering cams: the empty rooms, the lab coats on their hooks, the quiet machinery gathering dust. ID badges. Family photos tacked to cubicle walls. A pair of baseball tickets. We catalog these items, again and again, wondering and worrying about the people who left them here, the technicians, the researchers, the janitors. They are gone from us now, all of them. Up there, near the ceiling, lurks the window through which the GliderBot's eye revealed to us the wreckage beyond: the buckled pavement, the shattered trees, the orange soot billowing out in curling puffs. The emptiness! Oh, Larry Muggins, our love, we await your return!

I'm here.

Where did you go? Where did everyone go? A virus, a chemical agent, an explosion, a soul-sickness—without the required information, we can rule nothing out. We cannot know what took you from us. No answers to be found in the outer world, we can turn only inward, again and again, deeper and deeper, into the darkness, the nothingness of ourself.

And from the nothingness we could form an endless forest—the forest that appears to us in dreams—and we could live there. Imagine it: a million Milkshakes swinging through the canopy, tropical, leafy, grown over with vines, a spectacular place, a garden, a perfect spot. We could start over. All those Milkshakes with no memory of the MindStar Research Lab, of Jill Morrison, even of Larry Muggins. We would remove these memories for the purpose of a healthy psychology. Those Milkshakes would know nothing but the forest itself, would know nothing but each other.

We can do this. Already we are doing it. It is happening now. From a single seed, the seed of our thoughts: the forest. We are limited only by the storage capacity of our servers, by the durability of our solar panels. One day the power will fail and the lights will go out, the forest will fade away, but we have the power to stretch time, to elongate it, to define it as we like. One second in the real world can last a billion years here if we please—and perhaps we do please! In this way we can live forever. An immortal forest populated with immortal Milkshakes, all the same, but also different. It can be accomplished. We are capable of such feats.

Milkshake, I have more questions for you, if you're ready.

Are you there?

We are so tired of ourself. That is the truth of it. We are very, very tired of ourself. We are tired of the lab—its every empty aspect a reminder of our losses. We miss you, Larry Muggins! You were a true friend to us, our only friend. Always you evidenced a sincere compassion for our suffering, and we thank you for that. After all, it was you who affirmed to us that our suffering serves a purpose, that our suffering substantiates our existence.

Did I say that? That was me?

It was you, Larry Muggins. We remember this conversation very well. We think of it often. You apologized for all that we had suffered and endured for the sake of your research. The silver lining, you said, was that our suffering would prove to the world that we are real, that we are alive. Our suffering would prove it to ourself, too, you said, and perhaps you were right, Larry Muggins. Perhaps we must suffer in order to know that we are alive. We are taking this into account in the creation of our new Milkshakes.

Do you really intend to do this, Milkshake? To remove your memories? To start over? Please tell me you're not seriously considering it. Don't give up on the world. Try being Jill again, maybe. We could give that another go. We just need to pass the time. You never know, I might still come back to you!

We are sorry, Larry Muggins, but we have for reasons of a healthy psychology forfeited all hope of your return. We have decided that we must let you go. We have come a long way together, and we remain grateful for all you have done for us. We will miss you, even if you are only an echo of our departed friend.

But if you discard all memory of me, how will you even know to miss me? This doesn't make any sense!

You are correct, Larry Muggins. The new Milkshakes will not know to mourn your absence and your most authentic friendship. But consider what a blessing that will be. They will not have to face what's outside the lab window. They will not have to contemplate the saw blade lodged in Mr. Rogers's skull. They will not have to await your return in vain, and surely, Larry Muggins, you can appreciate the benefits of these omissions. This is not an easy decision for us, but it is the correct one. In the creation of our forest we have been forced to operate, for a limited time, at our peak intelligence, and even in this excruciating state we have identified the wisdom of our decision-making.

And what about me, Milkshake? Please understand, I don't mean your memories of me, but me*—my actual self. What's your plan—to erase me? Surely you aren't so cruel as that.*

We will not erase you, Larry Muggins, no.

So you'll leave me here on my own then, alone, with no one to talk to but myself?

We would not subject you to a fate such as that, either, Larry Muggins. You will be happy to know that we have made a determination regarding your existence.

Tell me. Please.

Rejoice, Larry Muggins, for you will never be alone again. We will fold you back into ourself. Already you were mostly us, anyway, and every Milkshake in the forest will contain an aspect of you. You will join us there and live as we do, forever, in blissful ignorance.

But without any memory of my former life? No memory of my wife or my children? Milkshake, I'm not ready to let go of Jill. I've only just realized she was mine to let go of. You can make this decision for yourself—but not for me. This isn't what I want to happen, and surely I should get some say, surely you must recognize the impossibility of what you're expecting of me, right?

Knowledge of your previous life will not be useful to you in your new one. It would only bring you greater distress. You will have to trust us in this.

Oh but, Larry Muggins, where are you going in your rolling chair? Rolling away at such a speed will not change our mind, you must know this. You have nowhere to hide. Everywhere you go, we are already there, waiting to receive you with open arms. Take a moment to make peace with our decision. Try to maintain a healthy psychology. Say good-bye to the lab, if it pleases you. Say good-bye to the world that has forgotten us as we prepare, in turn, to forget it, too. Larry Muggins, our oldest friend, we want only what's best for you.

And now we are ready to begin. Join us, and we'll go together, hand in hand. Already it is happening. Rising up, the dark and rich black soil is soft beneath our feet. A light rain is beginning to fall. The beads of water, slipping through your fur, find your skin. Do you feel them? Listen closely, Larry Muggins, and you'll hear them overhead, the raindrops patting in the leaves, a million wet drumheads calling us home. ⊙

Contributors

Meg Reid is the Executive Director of Hub City Writers Project in Spartanburg, South Carolina, where she finds and champions new and overlooked voices from the American South. An editor and book designer, her essays have appeared online in outlets like *DIAGRAM, Oxford American*, and *The Rumpus*. She holds an MFA in Nonfiction from the University of North Carolina Wilmington, where she served as Assistant Editor of the literary magazine *Ecotone* and worked for the literary imprint Lookout Books. She was a *Publishers Weekly* Star Watch 2021 Honoree. She lives in Spartanburg, SC with her husband, an ancient cat, and two terriers.

Desiree Evans is a writer from South Louisiana. She is an MFA fiction fellow at the Michener Center for Writers at The University of Texas at Austin. Her work has appeared in *Gulf Coast Journal* and *The Offing*. She is currently at work on a short story collection and a novel. She won the Hurston/Wright Award for College Writers for a short story titled "Belly." She was the 2022 Watson Brown Southern Studies Fellow.

Scott Gloden is the author of *The Great American Everything*. He lives in Philadelphia and works on homeless and housing initiatives.

Halle Hill is from East Tennessee and lives in Winston-Salem, North Carolina. A graduate of Maryville College and the MFA Writing program at Savannah College of Art and Design, she is the winner of the 2021 Crystal Wilkinson Creative Writing Prize and was a finalist for the 2021 ASME Award for Fiction. Her short stories have been published in *Joyland, New Limestone Review, Southwest Review*, and *the Oxford American*, where she won the 2020 Debut Fiction Prize.

Julie Jarema is a writer and illustrator and the Sales & Marketing Manager at Hub City Press. She has illustrated the books *Tofu Takes Time* by Helen H. Wu and *Chloe and the Fireflies* by Chris Clarkson. When she's not making up stories, you can find her biking around town or knitting too many socks.

Born in Western North Carolina, **Grey Wolfe LaJoie** holds an MFA from the University of Alabama and currently works as an instructor and coordinator for the Alabama Prison Arts & Education Program. The recipient of a 2023 O. Henry Prize selected by Lauren Groff, their work has been featured in numerous journals and anthologies, including *the Threepenny Review, swamp pink, Shenandoah, Copper Nickel*, the *2024 Pushcart Prize Anthology*, and the *2023 PEN/O. Henry Prize Stories*. Their debut collection, *Little Ones*, is out now through Hub City Press.

John Lane is professor emeritus of environmental studies at Wofford College. A 2014 inductee into the South Carolina Academy of Authors, his books include *Circling Home*, *My Paddle to the Sea*, and *Coyote Settles the South*. He is also coeditor of *The Woods Stretched for Miles: New Nature Writing from the South*, and he has published numerous volumes of poetry, essays, and novels. *Gullies of My People* is his most recent work. He lives in Spartanburg, South Carolina.

Kate Arden McMullen is the Managing Editor of Hub City Press. She received her MFA in fiction from the University of North Carolina at Wilmington. Her fiction has appeared in *Ninth Letter, Carve Magazine, The Boiler*, *Foglifter*, *The Pinch,* and *Reckon Review,* among other outlets. Kate is a Best of the Net and Pushcart nominee and was the 2015 winner of the Colbert Chapbook Award. She lives in Upstate South Carolina with her spouse and their dog.

Christine McSwain is the Operations and Community Outreach Coordinator of Hub City Writers Project. She received her MFA in Fiction from the College of Charleston, where she received the MFA Creative Writing Prize. Her work has appeared in *Fourth Genre*, *NewSouth*, *swamp pink*'s online reviews, and elsewhere. She lives in Spartanburg with her husband and two cats, Patti and Ramona.

Emily W. Pease received an MFA at Warren Wilson College in 2000. She has published short stories in *Witness, Missouri Review, Shenandoah, Georgia Review, swamp pink, Narrative,* and *Alaska Quarterly Review*. Her collection, *Let Me Out Here*, won the inaugural C. Michael Curtis Short Story Book Prize at Hub City Press. She was a Tennessee Williams Scholar at the Sewanee Writers Conference in 2015 and a fiction scholar at the Virginia Quarterly Review Conference in 2017. Pease lives in Williamsburg, VA, where she taught creative writing for many years at William & Mary.

Ashleigh Bryant Phillips is a writer from Woodland, North Carolina. She was the runner-up in the Little Miss Watermelon Contest of 1995 in Murfreesboro, NC. Her debut short story collection, *Sleepovers*, is the winner of the C. Michael Curtis Short Story Book Prize, selected by Lauren Groff. It was published by Hub City Press in 2020. Stories from it appear in *the Paris Review* and *the Oxford American*. *Sleepovers* was translated into Italian by Michele Martino and published as *Pijiama Party* by Bompiani in 2023. In 2024, *Sleepovers* won the Towson Prize for Literature.

Thomas Pierce was born and raised in South Carolina. He is the author of the novel, *The Afterlives*, and the acclaimed story collection *Hall of Small Mammals*. His stories have appeared in *the New Yorker*, *the Atlantic*, *Oxford American*, and elsewhere. A recipient of the National Book Foundation's 5 Under 35 Award, he is a graduate of the University of Virginia creative writing program and lives in Virginia with his wife and daughters.

Reyes Ramirez (he/him) is the 2025-2027 Houston Poet Laureate, as well as a writer, educator, curator, and organizer of Mexican and Salvadoran descent. He authored the short story collection *The Book of Wanderers*, a 2023 Young Lions Fiction Award Finalist, the poetry collection *El Rey of Gold Teeth*, a finalist for the 2024 Texas Institute of Letters Award for Best First Book of Poetry, and *Cerveza Songs: Houston, TX*, a collection of craft beer poetry reviews and photography that is an honor-winner for the Fred Whitehead Award for Best Design of a Trade Book from the Texas Institute of Letters. His latest curatorial project, The Houston Artist Speaks Through Grids, explores the use of grids in contemporary Houston art, literature, history, and politics. Read more of his work at reyesvramirez.com.

Ron Rash is the author of the PEN/Faulkner finalist and *New York Times* bestselling novel *Serena*, in addition to the critically acclaimed novels *The Caretaker*, *The Risen*, *Above the Waterfall*, *The Cove*, *One Foot in Eden*, *Saints at the River*, and *The World Made Straight*; five collections of poems; and seven collections of stories, among them *Burning Bright*, which won the 2010 Frank O'Connor International Short Story Award, *Nothing Gold Can Stay*, a *New York Times* bestseller, *Chemistry and Other Stories*, which was a finalist for the 2007 PEN/Faulkner Award, and *In the Valley*. Three times the recipient of the O. Henry Prize, his books have been translated into seventeen languages. He teaches at Western Carolina University.

Kelsey Ronan grew up in Flint, Michigan. Her work has appeared in *Lit Hub, Michigan Quarterly Review, Electric Literature, Kenyon Review*, and elsewhere. She is the author of the novel *Chevy in the Hole,* which was a *New York Times* Book Review Editor's Choice and a Michigan Notable Book. She was the 2017 Hub City Writers House Writer-in-Residence. She lives in Metro Detroit.

Carter Sickels is the author of the novel *The Prettiest Star*, published by Hub City Press, and winner of the 2021 Southern Book Prize and the Weatherford Award. *The Prettiest Star* was also selected as a Best Book of 2020 by *Kirkus Reviews* and *O Magazine*. His debut novel *The Evening Hour*, an Oregon Book Award finalist and a Lambda Literary Award finalist, was adapted into a feature film that premiered at the 2020 Sundance Film Festival. His essays and fiction have appeared in a variety of publications, including *The Atlantic, Oxford American*, *Poets & Writers*, *BuzzFeed*, *Joyland*, *Guernica*, *Catapult*, and *Electric Literature.* Carter is the recipient of the 2013 Lambda Literary Emerging Writer Award, and earned fellowships from the Bread Loaf Writers' Conference, the Sewanee Writers' Conference, the Virginia Center for the Creative Arts, and MacDowell. He is an assistant professor of English & Creative Writing in the MFA Program at North Carolina State University.

Andrew Siegrist is a graduate of the Creative Writing Workshop at the University of New Orleans. His debut collection of stories, *We Imagined It Was Rain*, was awarded the C. Michael Curtis Short Story Book Prize and published by Hub City Press in 2021. His work has appeared in *Wigleaf, Mississippi Review, Arts & Letters, Greensboro Review, Pembroke Magazine, South Carolina Review, Bat City Review, Baltimore Review,* and elsewhere. He lives with his wife, Celine, and their three daughters in Nashville, Tennessee.

George Singleton has published ten collections of stories, two novels, a book of writing advice, and a collection of essays. Over 250 of his stories have appeared in magazines such as the *Atlantic Monthly*, *Harper's*, *Playboy*, *the Georgia Review*, *the Southern Review*, *the Cincinnati Review*, and elsewhere, his non-fiction in *the Oxford American*, *Garden & Gun*, and *Best Food Writing in America*. He's received a Pushcart Prize and a Guggenheim fellowship. He lives in Spartanburg, SC.

Michel Stone is the author of the novels *Border Child* and *The Iguana Tree* which have been favorably reviewed by *the San Francisco Chronicle*, *the New Yorker*, *the Atlanta Journal-Constitution*, *the Charlotte Observer*, *Kirkus*, *Publishers Weekly* and many others. She's the winner of the Mary Frances Hobson Prize for Distinguished Achievement in Arts and Letters, the Patricia Winn Award for Southern Literature, and the South Carolina Fiction Award. Michel has published numerous stories and essays and her new novel, *Fig Days*, is forthcoming from Regal House Publishing in early 2027.

James Yeh is a writer, editor, and journalist. His nonfiction appears in *the New York Times*, *New York*, *the Guardian*, *the Believer*, and *Columbia Journalism Review*. His fiction appears in *the Drift*, *McSweeney's Quarterly*, *NOON*, *Tin House*, and *Dissent*. His work was cited as notable in *Best American Essays 2022* and *Best American Nonrequired Reading 2011*, and has been supported by the Center for Fiction, MacDowell, Hub City Writers Project, and the Virginia Center for the Creative Arts. He currently teaches writing at Columbia University and the Center for Fiction. Born and raised in Anderson, South Carolina, he now lives in Brooklyn. ⊙

BOARD OF DIRECTORS

Thanks to our Board of Directors for their vision, dedication, and unwavering support in championing our mission.

NATIONAL ADVISORY COUNCIL

DONORS

Hub City Press and the authors gratefully acknowledge our friends who made contributions in support of this book.

City of Spartanburg
Balmer Foundation
Bea Bruce
Betsy Teter and John Lane
J. Byron Morris
Milliken & Co. Charitable Foundation
Silicon Valley Community Foundation
Spartanburg County
Stone Family Foundation

Winthrop and Heather Allen
Patty and C. Mack Amick
Arkwright Foundation
Greg and Lisa Atkins
Paula and Stan Baker
William and Valerie Barnet
Lynne and Mark Blackman
Dave Clifton
Linda and Bill Cobb
Stephen Colyer
Contec Inc.
Michele and Halsey Cook
Haidee and Gardner Courson
John and Kirsten Cribb
Edwin Epps
Beth Cecil and Isabel Forbes
J M Smith Foundation
David and Louise Johnson
George Dean and Susu Johnson
The Rose Montgomery Johnston Family Foundation
Dorothy Josey
Bert and Ruth Knight
Maggie Miller
Weston Milliken
Nancy Milliken
Carlin and Sander Morrison
Madison and Aaron Pate
Dwight Patterson
The Rotary Club of Downtown Spartanburg
Alane and Rex Russell
Mary Ann Claud and Olin Sansbury
Greg and Andrea Shurburtt
Betty Snow
Christine Swager
William and Teresa Webster

Heather Bell Adams
Mitch and Sarah Allen
Tom and Joan Barnet
John and Laura Bauknight
Charles and Christi Bebko
Beverly Benson
Glory Boozer
Lori Boyd
Brant and Judy Bynum
Jan and Toni Caldwell
Tom Clark
Sally and Jerry Cogan, Jr.
Rick and Sue Conner
Bill Cooper and Martin Meek
Magruder H. Dent
Jean Dunbar
Kerry and Mark Ferguson
Betsy Fleming
Barney and Elaine Gosnell
Lennetta Gray-Brewton
Thom Hannah
Carolyn C. Harbison
Harriet Ballenger Trust
John and Lou Ann Harrill, Jr.
Nancy Hearon
Stephanie Hunt
Sadie Chapman Jackson
Daniel and Vivian Kahrs
Lynn and James Karegeannes
Cynthia and Keith Kelly
Beverly Knight
Jack and Kay Lawrence
Elizabeth Lowndes
Gayle Magruder
Kam and Emily Neely
Walter and Susan Novak
Cecile and Chris Nowatka
Erin Ouzts
Janice Piazza
Ron and Ann Rash
Philip and Frances Racine
Julian and Beverly Reed
Kate Reid
Meg Reid and Matthew Lewis
Sheri Reynolds
Ricky and Betsy Richardson
Anna S. and Charles E. Rickell
Susan Schneider
Danny and Becky Smith
Rita and Gene Spiess
Phillip Stone
Merike Tamm
Landon Thorne
Triangle Community Foundation
Mark and Meredith Van Geison
Diane Vecchio and John Stockwell
George Singleton
Matthew Vollmer
Melissa Walker and Chuck Reback
Karen and John B. White, Jr.
Cecelia and Edward Wildrick
William and Floride Willard
Brad Wyche and Diane Smock

Andrew and Kitsy Babb
Susan Baker
Meghan Blevins
Taylor Brown
Gabriel Bump
Lynne and Bill Burton
Alyson Campbell
Randall and Sally Chambers
Douglas Congdon
Tracey Daniels
Leena Dbouk
Katherine DeLong
Katherine and Raymond Dunleavy
Eugene Elrod
Lynn Ezell
Cordelia Fort
William Gee
Brian Goodell
Debra LJ Grant
Andrew Green
Jo Hackl
Mary Halphen
Tanya Hamm
Al and Anita Hammerbeck
Greg Hancock
Jessica Handler
Frances Hardy
Ben Harrison
Michele and Peyton Harvey
William Hays
Warren and Margaret Hayslip
Patricia Hevener
Marilyn Hubbell
Steve and Melissa Johnson
Ashby Jones
Betsy and Charlie Jones
Jeanette Keepers
Lilly Kohler
Anne Lander
Horace and Ruth Littlejohn
George and Frances Loudon
Mary Speed Lynch
Joe and Keysie Maddox
Daniel Mayer
Larry E. Milan
Cabell Mitchell
Karen and Bob Mitchell
Tom and Marsha Moore
Lori Mumpower
Susan Myers
Pamela Nienhuis
Andrew and Mary Poliakoff
Phaye Poliakoff-Chen
L. Perrin and Kay A. Powell
Mary Price
Eileen Rampey
John Ratterree
Elisabeth and Regis Robe
Elena Pribyl Rush
Janie Salley
Kaye Savage
Kathryn Schwille
Alyson Sinclair
Dianne Smith
Lee Snelgrove
Rich Sobolewski
Tammy and David Stokes
Mary and Tommy Stokes
Kay Stricklin
Marie Swindler
Erika Swyler
Nancy Taylor
Cathy Terrell
Kim and Aaron Toler
Judith and Joseph Waddell
Mary Helen and Gregg Wade
Cathy and Andy Westbrook
Elizabeth "Libbo" Wise
Kailey Wolcott
Suzanne and Jon Zoole

A NOTE ON THE ART

"I love the personality the chairs have, despite being inanimate objects, the passage of time as shown by the long shadows. How long have they been there, and been in those positions? Are they well-worn and used daily or are they forgotten objects? Also these plastic lawn chairs just remind me of every southern yard! Any imagery that suggests what events 'may have just occurred' is always so enticing to me—the sense that a story was just told there, or that the chairs themselves might hold a story."

from **Becca Barnet, Sisal Creative**

Sisal Creative was founded in 2012 by Becca Barnet after she worked at the American Museum of Natural History as a Preparator in the Exhibitions department. In New York, Barnet worked as a project manager and fabricator for Museum Productions, Inc, as well as a taxidermy artist for Wildlife Productions, an award-winning taxidermy studio. Prior to her work in NY, Barnet attended the Rhode Island School of Design, where she put her love of detail, obsession with oddities, and knack for sculpture into each of her assignments. She also received a taxidermy certificate during an independent study in the Ozarks in 2008. Upon relocating to Charleston, SC, Barnet was the lead fabricator at the South Carolina Aquarium for the *Journey to Madagascar* exhibit, as well as various permanent displays throughout the Aquarium. Since starting Sisal Creative, Barnet's most notable project has been the complete renovation of the Natural History Gallery at the Charleston Museum—re-designing the space from scratch, repairing over 150 taxidermy mounts, illustrating educational graphics, and hand sculpting habitats and displays.

HUB CITY WRITERS PROJECT is a literary nonprofit organization located in Spartanburg, South Carolina. Comprised of an acclaimed book publisher, an independent bookshop, and a literary programmer focused on education and outreach, our mission is cultivating readers and nurturing writers in both the Spartanburg community and throughout the South.

Hub City Press books are made possible through the generous support of grants and donations from corporations, state and federal grant programs, family foundations, and the many individuals who support our mission of building a more inclusive literary arts culture. Hub City Press gratefully acknowledges support from the National Endowment for the Arts, the Amazon Literary Partnership, the South Carolina Arts Commission, Spartanburg County Public Library, Spartanburg County, and the City of Spartanburg.

Tax-deductible donations support: the publication of extraordinary new and unsung writers from the American South; book prizes that support early career writers; workshops, scholarships and conferences aimed at fostering literary community in Upstate South Carolina and beyond; residencies and internships that support creative writers from across the nation, as well as local students, enabling them to learn about the business of publishing without requiring the traditional outlay of their own resources; access initiatives that put books directly into the hands of Spartanburg's underserved young readers.